URBAN UNDERGROUND

SADDLEBACK
EDUCATIONAL PUBLISHING
www.sdlback.com

ISBN-13: 978-1-61651-270-5
ISBN-10: 1-61651-270-9
eBook: 978-1-60291-995-2

Printed in Guangzhou, China
1010/10-25-10

16 15 14 13 12   1 2 3 4 5

CHAPTER ONE

Sixteen-year-old Ernesto Sandoval was buying an apple from the vending machine at Cesar Chavez High School when Carmen Ibarra came running up to him. She was a good friend of Ernesto's, but she wasn't his girlfriend. Naomi Martinez was the girl Ernesto loved.

"Ernie! Ernie! Ernie!" Carmen yelled. "My dad is running for city council!"

Ernesto smiled. Carmen could talk more and louder than anybody else he knew. She was very excitable. Everybody liked Carmen because she had your back when you were in trouble.

"That's great, Carmen," Ernesto said. "We need a good person in there."

1

Emilio Zapata Ibarra, Carmen's father, was a larger-than-life character. At Carmen's parties, he wore a plastic sheriff's badge from a cereal box. But nearly all his neighbors had stories of when he reached out to them with advice, money, or comfort in times of need. Ibarra defended the streets from gangbangers and drug dealers. He worked with veterans' organizations and programs for the homeless, seniors, and teenagers.

"Yeah," Carmen went on, "the guy who's in there now, that Monte Esposito, he's a big bag of wind. He likes to get on television and talk about all his big plans, but he doesn't do anything. He's been in almost ten years, and he's done nothing. Problems that our *barrio* people took to him when he first got elected are still on the back-burner. Like that gangbanger hangout on Starling—the creeps are using it again. Some of the parents on that street have gone to Esposito for help, and his assistant says, 'He's studying the problem.'

The place needs to be condemned. If my dad gets elected, he'll take care of business."

"Yeah, I believe it," Ernesto agreed, grinning. He was a little afraid of Mr. Ibarra, but clearly the man had a passion for justice and a sincere desire to help people. That was clearly not the case with Esposito. He was an entrenched politician who became less effective every year.

Naomi Martinez came walking over. "What's going on, Carmen? What's all the excitement about?" she inquired.

"My dad's gonna run for the city council to unseat Monte Esposito," Carmen bubbled. "Oh, there's so much he wants to do for the people around here. He wants to have an open-door policy so anybody with a problem can come in and talk to him. With Esposito, you have to like wait three months just to see his assistant!"

Naomi grew very quiet. Then she spoke. "Monte Esposito is my dad's cousin.

They grew up together, and they're very close now. Dad really likes Monte. He gets perks and shares them with Dad, like tickets to the football games."

Carmen's eyes grew very large. "Oh, I didn't even know that, Naomi," she responded.

"Yeah," Naomi said. Her father, Felix Martinez, was a tough man who could be harsh. He domineered Naomi's mother. He bought a pit bull a few months ago. Even though his wife was terrified of the animal, he forced her to accept it. His wife, Linda Martinez, locked herself in the kitchen when the dog was loose, and she trembled with fear. Now she was used to the dog— Brutus. She even liked him, but for a while living in her own home was terrible for Mrs. Martinez

Ernesto felt weird. He loved Naomi, and he really liked Carmen. Ernesto's father, Luis Sandoval, taught history at Chavez High, and Ernesto had heard a lot of political talk around the dinner table.

Dad often mentioned that Monte Esposito didn't serve the people in the *barrio*. He served himself and his cronies.

"Esposito keeps his chair warm down there at city council, but that's about it," Ernesto's dad would say. "We were trying to get a traffic light installed across from Veterans Hall. That way, some of those poor older guys don't have to risk life and limb crossing at that dangerous intersection. But Esposito just stonewalled us. He's been asleep at the wheel for a long time."

Ernesto and his family had just moved back into the *barrio* a short time ago. For ten years they had lived in Los Angeles. So Ernesto didn't know too much about local politics. His father, though, had kept in touch with friends he'd known in town since childhood.

Ernesto looked at Naomi and told her, "Your dad's cousin will probably be re-elected. People usually vote for the person who's in."

"Yeah," Carmen fumed, her eyes catching fire. "That's the problem. After you get elected, you don't have to do anything. They just keep on electing you. You can just sit there collecting your salary and let the *barrio* go to the dogs."

Naomi looked troubled. She was a bright student. She knew, as did everyone else, that Monte Esposito was a poor public servant. But she also knew how close her father was to the man. Naomi's father didn't take kindly to family members defying him. He had already kicked his two older sons, Orlando and Manny, out of the house just for standing up to him.

"Well," Carmen declared, "I'm going to do all I can to help my dad get elected. The club we've formed, me and my friends, it's called the *Zapatistas*. We're gonna canvas the neighborhood and talk to people, pass out flyers."

When Carmen walked away, Ernesto said to Naomi, "Well, I've never liked politics much."

Naomi shrugged. "Last time Monte Esposito ran for reelection, I helped paint posters for his campaign. Me and Zack worked hard. We even had little parties at our house to raise money for him."

"Uh, do *you* like the guy, Naomi?" Ernesto asked carefully.

"I don't know," Naomi answered. "My brother Zack said he's a crook. Zack didn't say that around Dad, though. Zack pretends he likes him. I guess Monte is Dad's claim to fame. When the councilman goes to some big party, he always invites my parents. And they get to sit with the big shots. I think Dad would feel really bad if Esposito lost the election and wasn't a councilman anymore."

Ernesto was a little nervous. Deep in his heart he knew that Monte Esposito was not good for the *barrio*. Rumors even went around that the guy was a crook. Ernesto thought that Carmen's father would do a lot of good in the community but wasn't about to upset Naomi. So he kept his mouth shut.

Nothing meant more to Ernesto than Naomi. Ernesto hoped that Carmen Ibarra wouldn't expect him to join the *Zapatistas*. He just couldn't.

Later that day, Ernesto had lunch with his best friend, Abel Ruiz. Abel was the first kid who reached out when Ernesto first came on campus as a stranger. Also at lunch were two teammates from the Chavez Cougar track team that Ernesto belonged to, Julio Avila and Jorge Aguilar.

"Carmen is really charged up about her dad running for city council, huh?" Abel asked. "That girl is hotter than a jalapeno pepper. With her working for her dad, he's a sure thing to get elected."

"Yeah," Ernesto replied. "Emilio Ibarra is a good man, that's for sure."

"Esposito got in some trouble last year for going to the Bahamas on our tax money," said Jorge Aguilar. "But he weaseled out of that somehow."

Ernesto didn't want to hear that. It was bad enough that Monte Esposito was not a good councilman. If he was also dishonest, that bothered Ernesto. The thought that he wouldn't help to elect a good, honest man made him feel guilty—that he'd rather see the inept crook remain in place just so his girlfriend wouldn't be upset. Ernesto felt like a creep, and he hated the feeling.

"I guess there's always gossip about people," Ernesto commented in a lame voice. "Esposito probably isn't any worse than the other politicians we got in there."

"My dad, he's a war veteran, you know," Julio chimed in. "And he's got a buddy, calls him Rezzi. He's a vet too. Rezzi used to work for Esposito. He's told Dad stuff about Esposito that'd turn a guy's curly hair straight. That's what my dad said."

Ernesto often saw Julio's dad at the track meets. He wore old, threadbare clothing, and he looked as though life had stomped on him pretty hard. But Mr. Avila was proud of Julio. When Julio won a race, as he often did, the man beamed with pride. Julio was his only child, his only relative.

His mother was long dead. Mr. Avila said his only reason for living was to see his son be successful. Maybe one day, Mr. Avila hoped, Julio would go the Olympics and win a gold medal.

"My grandpa was a vet," Jorge said. "And he's really old now. He says a lot of veterans hang out in the ravine 'cause they're homeless. Grandpa wrote a letter to Esposito asking him if the city could do something to reach out to these guys. Grandpa's doing okay. He lives with us. But the other guys, some of them have nowhere to go. You'd think something could be done. But Esposito never answered the letter. I guess he had better things to do, like hanging out in the Bahamas and playing golf with his fat cat *amigos*."

The boys laughed and finished their lunches. Ernesto didn't laugh. He always prided himself on having the courage to do the right thing. Luis Sandoval, his dad, walked the *barrio*. He struck up conversations with dropouts and even gangbangers, trying to turn their lives around. He did that even though it was dangerous, and Ernesto was intensely proud of him for doing that.

Ernesto didn't feel very proud of himself.

Carmen then showed up. "Hi guys. I know it's against school rules to pass out any campaign literature on campus. But I got a lot of really great brochures telling what my dad will do if he's elected. I got the flyers in my binder, and I'll give you a couple. But make sure you keep them out of sight. No campaigning on campus. That's what Ms. Sanchez says, and she's the principal. She makes the rules."

Ernesto took one of the flyers. It showed a color photograph of Emilio Zapata Ibarra, a big, burly man with a handlebar mustache. Ernesto remembered the first time he met him at a party at Carmen's house. He had a very intimidating presence. He had already established a neighborhood watch on Nuthatch Lane. Since then, the crime rate had plunged. Where burglaries had been common, they were now rare. The gangbangers and the dopeheads avoided Nuthatch Lane because of the big man with the mustache.

Julio took a flyer too. "It looks great," he remarked, stuffing it into his history book.

"Sounds like this is the guy we need," Jorge Aguilar affirmed.

By the end of the school day, Ernesto needed to talk with someone about his dilemma. Abel, Ernesto's best friend, was the perfect choice. Ernesto lived on Wren Street, and Abel lived three streets down on Sparrow. While they walked home from school together, as they often did, Ernesto confided in Abel.

"Abel, you know how great things are going now for Naomi and me," Ernesto began. "I mean, I liked her the minute I met her, but I never dreamed we'd ever be together. I thought she'd be with Clay forever, and I didn't have a chance. Now everything is so good between us. I don't want anything to ruin that, y'hear what I'm saying? I'd like Carmen's dad to win that election, but I don't want to get involved. Esposito is related to Naomi's dad—a cousin—and his buddy too. If I got mixed up supporting Ibarra, it'd get back to Felix Martinez and make a problem for us—for Naomi and me."

"I hear you man," Abel sympathized. "My dad says all politics are dirty, that ordinary people should stay out of it." Abel's father worked as a laborer for a landscaping business. He didn't believe in making waves over anything. He just did what his wife told him to do and kept his head down.

Ernesto sighed. His own father didn't feel that way. Ernesto's dad believed every citizen had the duty to be well informed and to fight for good government. Ernesto would have been embarrassed to tell his dad how he really felt. His heart and his conscience told him Ibarra was the best man for city council. But keeping his girlfriend happy was more important.

"That guy, Monte Esposito, you ever meet him?" Ernesto asked, as the boys walked.

"Nah," Abel responded. "He don't bother with people like us. Don't stress about it, dude. We're just the little *peons*. We can't do much about anything. That's what Dad says."

Ernesto was a simple sixteen-year-old guy. He worked hard to keep up his grades at Chavez, ran on the track team, and worked for Bashar at the pizzeria. He didn't want any problems. That was the bottom line. He was Naomi's boyfriend, and she meant the world to him. The difference between a blah weekend and a blast was whether Naomi was riding somewhere with him in his Volvo.

"I seen lots of pictures of Esposito," Abel added, chuckling. "He's a big guy, got a beer belly. He's like everybody's idea of a crooked politician. Smokes big cigars. If you want somebody to play a political jerk in a bad movie, you'd pick him."

"Well, he keeps getting elected," Ernesto commented. "So somebody must like him."

"He had some good ideas when he first got in, but then he got lazy, I guess," Abel said.

"Well, it's none of my business," Ernesto declared. The moment the words were out of his mouth, Ernesto felt guilty again. He was saying that he didn't care if the *barrio* had a bad councilman.

When Ernesto got home, his mother, Maria Sandoval, was talking about when her picture book was being published. Ernesto's mother was a stay-at-home mom, and she had never done anything unusual before. But now she had written a picture book, and the printed copies would be arriving soon. Mom was very excited. So were Katalina and Juanita, Ernesto's little sisters.

Eight-year-old Katalina told her mom, "I'm gonna show your book to everybody in third grade."

Not to be outdone, six-year-old Juanita looked up from the jigsaw puzzle she was working on with *Abuela* Lena. "I'm gonna show it to everybody in first grade," she announced, "and ask my teacher to read it to the class."

When Ernesto put his books down on the table, Katalina spotted the colorful flyer lying on top of them. "What's this?" she asked, giggling. "Mama, Ernie has a colored picture of Carmen's daddy!"

"Oh," Ernesto replied, "that's a political flyer."

Ernesto's mother came over to the table, picked up the flyer, and read it. "My, this is well done," she remarked. "No attacks on his opponent. Just a clear message of what he plans to do if elected. I was talking to Conchita about her husband running. I told her it'd turn their life upside down if he became a councilman. Conchita said they didn't care. They're both so fired up about doing some good in the *barrio*."

"Mom," Ernesto asked, "did you know that Monte Esposito is Felix Martinez's cousin?"

Maria Sandoval nodded yes. "Yes. I shouldn't say this, but I never liked Felix Martinez or his cousin. I remember them as boys tearing up the neighborhood. Very arrogant, I hope Mr. Ibarra gets in."

"Well," Ernesto declared, "I'm gonna stay out of it. I don't want friction between me and Naomi."

"Oh? Does Naomi think Monte Esposito is a good councilman?" Mom asked.

"Uh, I don't think so, Mom. But he's real close with her father and . . . You know how that goes," Ernesto said.

Abuela Lena was Luis Sandoval's widowed mother who had recently come to live with the Sandovals. She looked up from the jigsaw puzzle and spoke. "I remember years ago there was a councilman in the *barrio* named Harry Maynard. Mr. Maynard took a great interest in the young people. He contacted businesspeople and started a scholarship program for disadvantaged young people to go to college. It was such a blessing, and it never would have happened without his leadership. At the time my husband and I had these five children and not a lot of money. Luis and Arturo both got scholarships. Your father was able to become a teacher and Arturo a lawyer. The money helped our family very much. A good man like Mr. Maynard can make a difference in so many lives."

"Yeah," Ernesto recalled. "I remember Dad telling me about that. He always keeps a picture of Mr. Maynard on the wall in the den."

Maria Sandoval was still reading the flyer. "Oh look, Mama. Emilio wants to bring that scholarship program back. The one Mr. Maynard started. It was called the Nicolo Sena Scholarship. It was named for a Mexican-American boy from the *barrio* who died in the Vietnam War."

"That would be wonderful," *Abuela* exclaimed. "Mr. Esposito showed no interest in it, and it died on the vine."

Ernesto headed for his room. He got on his computer and did some research for

Ms. Hunt's English class. She was an excellent teacher, but very demanding and Ernesto wanted an A in her class.

Ernesto didn't care for Felix Martinez, Naomi's father. Ernesto spent as little time as possible at the Martinez house. For one thing, Martinez was always putting his wife, Linda, down, calling her "stupid" and "idiot." And Mrs. Martinez seemed to take the treatment without complaint. On rare occasions, Felix even hit her. But she accepted the violence too, as part of her lot. Linda Martinez loved her husband, and she believed he loved her. Ernesto didn't know whether Mr. Martinez loved his wife, but Ernesto hated how he treated her. Ernesto was tempted to campaign for Emilio Ibarra. He wanted to. Helping was the right thing to do.

Ernesto's hands formed into fists. They were so tight his fingers hurt. He pounded his fists on the side of his chair in frustration.

Every time Ernesto made up his mind to campaign for Emilio Zapata Ibarra, all he could see were Naomi's amazing violet eyes and her sweet face. She was a good person. She was kind and compassionate. But she loved her father with all his faults. If Ernesto took sides against her father's cousin, he would only hurt her. Naomi would be in a terrible place. She'd be caught in the middle between the boy she loved and the father she cared for and respected.

Ernesto just couldn't do that.

CHAPTER TWO

When Ernesto was working at the pizzeria the next afternoon, Clay Aguirre came in alone. Naomi and Clay had been friends since middle school and dated for a couple of years at Chavez. Naomi had been with Ernesto only in the last few months. Clay and Naomi might never have split if they hadn't gotten into an argument It ended with Clay punching Naomi in the face. Naomi had put up with Clay's rudeness for a long time because she cared for him. But hitting her was a deal breaker. Still, Ernesto noticed Clay often staring at Naomi, a longing in his eyes. In classes at Chavez High, Clay spent more time looking at Naomi than he did looking at the teachers.

Since Naomi had broken up with him, Clay'd been hanging with Mira Nuñez. But, when Clay came into the pizza store, she was nowhere to be seen. Ernesto had an uncomfortable feeling about Clay. He suspected that Clay hadn't given up on getting Naomi back. Poor Mira was just a ploy to make Naomi jealous. The trick didn't work on Naomi, of course.

Clay seemed to know that Naomi came into the shop every Wednesday night. When Ernesto went off his shift, he and Naomi would leave together. He'd drop her at her house before going home himself.

Shortly after Clay sat down with a pizza slice and cola, Naomi walked in. Clay hailed her. "Hey Naomi," Clay called to the girl. "I want to tell you something."

Naomi looked tense. Right after she'd broken up with Clay, he had followed her constantly to see what she was doing and who was with her. He was almost a stalker. One day Naomi warned Clay to stop it or she'd call the police. He did stop.

"Hello Clay," she responded now. "What do you want to tell me?"

"Me and my friends at Chavez are big supporters of Monte Esposito," Clay announced. "I just wanted you to know that Carmen thinks everybody at school is a *Zapatista*, but that's a crock. Lot of us are gonna work for your dad's cousin."

"Oh," Naomi replied. "Well, thanks for telling me."

"Yeah, well," Clay went on, "we think Emilio Ibarra is kind of a clown with his fake sheriff's badge and stuff. Lotta people see him as a big fool. Councilman Esposito, he's got the experience, and he's good for the job." Clay was hoping that supporting Esposito would be a wedge for him to get back into her life.

"I like Carmen," Naomi told him. "She's my friend. Her father's a good man. I just don't get into politics, but thanks anyway for telling me how you feel, Clay."

"Yeah, anytime," Clay said, returning to his pizza.

Naomi went to the counter and sat on one of the stools. "I'll just have a little salad, Ernie," she said. She seemed shaken by the encounter with Clay. For a long time she had thought she was in love with Clay Aguirre. Breaking up with him was very hard for her, and she was just recently getting comfortable in her new relationship with Ernie. But she remained polite to Clay. She could never completely forget their history, what they had once meant to each other.

Ernesto smiled at Naomi and asked her, "You pick a writer to do a report on yet for Ms. Hunt?" Ms. Hunt wanted each student to do a big multimedia presentation on a writer.

"Yeah, I'm doing mine on Eudora Welty," Naomi answered. "She made a lot of appearances on television talking about her books and her writing style. And I can use all that. I liked her stories, and she was such a down-to-earth lady."

"Yeah," Ernesto agreed, "I remember reading that one story about the little girl visiting the nursing home. It was realistic. No sugar coating there."

"'A Visit of Charity,' yeah," Naomi replied. "The story was disturbing, but that's what good writing should be. We need to be disturbed sometimes. It's nice to imagine a sweet little girl visiting some sweet old ladies. But the kid was cold, and the old ladies were anything but sweet. Life isn't always nice and sweet."

Clay continued to stare at Naomi as he sat at the corner table, nursing his cola. He never took his eyes off Naomi. He was making Ernesto angry and worried. Ernesto cared a lot about Naomi, but their relationship was new. Ernesto didn't feel totally confident about it yet.

"I'm probably gonna do my report on F. Scott Fitzgerald," Ernesto said. "He was such an interesting guy, and he died so young. I can use clips from that movie they made from his book, *The Great Gatsby*."

"That'll be terrific," Naomi responded. "When's your mom's book coming out?"

Ernesto smiled while he spoke. "Any day now. Believe me, since the pit bull in the story is based on your dog, Brutus, you guys'll get your copy right away. Mom is so excited about it."

"She should be," Naomi affirmed. "It's a big deal getting a book published." Naomi glanced back to where Clay was sitting. "I'd hoped he'd gone," she sighed wistfully.

Ernesto didn't know what to say. Did Clay's presence stir old memories that were painful to remember? Or was she anxious about his continued obsession with her?

Then Naomi confided, "The other day he sent me a card, a pretty, flowery card. It was for the anniversary of the first real date we had. We were freshmen at Chavez, and he took me to the movies. His father drove us. I had forgotten the date. And here comes this card, and I checked, and yes, he had the date right. It made me feel bad. I so wish he was over me, Ernie. I hate for him to continue to feel bad that we're not together."

Ernesto wanted to say all kinds of nasty things, but he thought he better not. He wanted to tell her that a power thing—a pride thing—had Clay mired in the past. He was a big, handsome, muscular guy. He always thought that he could have any chick he wanted and that she'd be glad to have him. That's why he took Naomi for granted and didn't treat her with respect. She had actually dumped him; she didn't want him anymore. That flew in the face of everything he believed about himself. He couldn't get over it. He couldn't come to terms with it. Ernesto knew that Naomi didn't see it that way. She thought he still loved her so much that he was hurting. That idea bothered her compassionate heart. She didn't see the ego part of it. And Ernesto did not want to go there for fear of offending her.

"Clay hangs with Mira Nuñez sometimes," Ernesto told her. The truth was that Clay and Mira were together very little. Once Clay realized the jealousy ploy wasn't working, he lost interest in Mira.

"No," Naomi said regretfully. "I don't think they're that into each other. I shouldn't care, but it bothers me that he can't get past this."

Soon it was time for Ernesto to go off his shift, and he pulled on his jacket. Clay was still sitting at the table, with an empty bottle of cola. Ernesto and Naomi had to walk past him on their way out. As they did, he looked up and said, "Goodnight, Naomi."

"Oh, goodnight, Clay," Naomi responded.

"Naomi," Clay said, "say 'Hi' to your dad for me. He's a great guy. I always enjoyed talking to him when I came to your house. He's a real man. A tough, no-nonsense kind of guy. Be sure to tell him that a lot of us'll be working for Monte Esposito. Tell him we'll get his cousin reelected. We won't let some upstart knock off a good man like him."

"I'll tell him, Clay," Naomi answered. She walked a little faster with Ernesto.

As they approached the Volvo, Naomi spoke. "Clay and my dad always got along

good. They're sorta alike. Dad liked him."
A pained look clouded Naomi's eyes.

"Even after . . . I mean, after Clay, you
know, hurt me. I thought my dad would be
furious with him, but he wasn't. Dad took
me aside. He said that sometimes a man has
to prove his love in harsh ways. I didn't
understand that. I didn't accept it. I came
close to being very angry with my dad at
the time. I mean, he tried to say that Clay
must love me very much. He got so angry
at the thought that I was admiring another
guy . . . he must love me so much that he
hit me."

"That's crazy," Ernesto commented, as
he opened the car door for her.

As the Volvo turned into the street,
Naomi asked a question that was on her
mind. "You think that if someone loves
you, they can't hurt you, Ernie?"

"Oh no, I'm not saying that," Ernesto
responded. "We hurt people we love all the
time. We say mean things, and we get impa-
tient. I mean, I love my little sister, Katalina,

a lot. But the other day she got into my research on Fitzgerald, and I yelled at her. She felt bad, and I felt bad. But hitting somebody, that's you know, unacceptable."

"I don't know," Naomi objected. "I'm taking that class in California history, and we're talking about the Spanish era. The ranchos. The father in the family, the ranchero, he used physical punishment against his grown sons. The son could be fifty, and the father could beat him. And that was all right. Nobody thought anything of it."

"Luckily, we've learned a lot since then, Naomi," Ernesto replied. "You aren't supposed to beat on other people, even family. You sure aren't supposed to hit a girl you love. Besides, this ranchero dude, he probably was punishing his kid for some misdeed or something. And he probably kept a tight rein on his emotions. But a boyfriend hitting his girlfriend in red hot anger, that could be really awful."

"Yeah, I hear you, Ernie," Naomi acceded.

Ernesto pulled into the driveway of the Martinez house on Bluebird Street. Felix Martinez was outside with the dog, Brutus. The dog followed him everywhere, its tail wagging. Everyone in the family loved Brutus, but he seemed to know who his best friend was—Dad. When Martinez went out in his pickup truck, he just whistled. Brutus jumped in beside him, sitting in the passenger seat. You'd see the pickup truck going down the street, Brutus poking his head out the window, looking around.

"Hey Ernie, how's it goin'?" Mr. Martinez called out cheerfully.

"Pretty good. I'm running in the track meet Wednesday," Ernesto answered, as he and Naomi got out of the car.

"Hey Ernie, you're looking bigger, more muscle. You oughta go out for football. Runnin' around in little short pants, that's not a sport for a guy," Felix chided, laughing.

"Well," Ernesto thought, "he insulted me again. It isn't the first time, and it won't be the last." Ernesto knew what he had to do out of respect for the girl he loved. Suck it up. He couldn't respond by saying what he was thinking. "Hey man, why don't you mind your own business? A lot of really great guys are on the track team. Some of the football players are jerks. It doesn't matter what sport you choose. It's not important man, so give it a rest."

"Well, to each his own," Ernesto replied out loud, blandly.

"Ernie," Mr. Martinez declared, "some kids down at your school're working for that idiot, Ibarra. They call themselves the *Zapatistas* if you can believe it. They want to get my cousin off the council. There never was a better man in there than Monte. He practically runs the whole town. The mayor, he don't do nothin' without consulting Monte."

"Uh-oh," Ernesto said inside his head, "then the mayor's a fool too. Or a crook." But aloud, Ernesto just said, "Yeah?"

"My boy Zack," the man went on, "he and some of his friends are working for

Monte. I'm trying to get Naomi on board, but she says she don't like politics. You need to start working for Monte, Ernie. We need kids like you to pass out absentee ballots to the old fogies who can't get to the polls."

"Oh, gotta get home," Ernesto said abruptly.

He waved good-bye and got back into the car. Naomi rushed into the house without saying anything to her father. Ernesto felt sorry for her. This election was harder on her than on him. He didn't have to live with Felix Martinez.

"Always nice seein' you, Ernie," Felix Martinez responded amiably. He was still in a pretty good mood. Naomi always said two beers made him sociable, and the third made him nasty.

As Ernesto backed out of the driveway, he almost hit a wooden sign on the lawn. He hadn't noticed it when he drove in. It was a red, white, and blue sign that bore the name "Esposito."

At Chavez High the next day, Ernesto was hurrying toward English class. Ms. Hunt had promised to come early so that students could get her approval of the authors they had chosen for their reports. Ernesto was really excited about F. Scott Fitzgerald, and he wanted to make sure she'd accept his selection.

As Ernesto walked toward English, Abel Ruiz fell in step beside him. "Well, I did it man. I joined the group working for Carmen's dad. The *Zapatistas*. I swore I wouldn't get involved, but it just got to me, Ernie. I'm dating Claudia now. She talked to me and convinced me. If we don't work for Ibarra, all the bad stuff this dude we got is doing will be our fault too."

"Well, good for you, Abel," Ernesto responded. "I'm staying out of the whole thing, though."

"I know you're in a bind because of Naomi man," Abel acknowledged. "But something Claudia said got me. Esposito's backing the mayor's plan to cut the police department by five percent and take some cops off the street. Dude, we had only three gang killings in the *barrio* last year. And the only reason it's better now is we got more cops." Abel was speaking passionately.

"Abel, I can't get mixed up in this, man," Ernesto protested, frustration coming into his voice.

Just then Julio Avila caught up with them. He heard the last part of the conversation between Ernesto and Abel.

"Mixed up in what, Ernie?" he asked.

"This city council election business," Ernesto answered. "I'm too busy with my classes and working at the pizza place. I'm already stressed," He didn't want to come right out with his real reason for not carrying water for Ibarra even though he believed in the cause.

Julio looked right at Ernesto and nodded toward the science building. "Good thing that guy didn't feel that way," he said.

"What guy?" Ernesto demanded, wanting to get to English so Ms. Hunt could approve Fitzgerald. He was annoyed at Julio for slowing him down.

"The guy the school is named for, man," Julio answered. "Look at the mural on the side of the science building, dude. The mural Dom and Carlos and the other kids made."

Ernesto knew the mural well. His father arranged for the kids to paint it.

"Look at old Cesar standing there with all those weary-looking men, women, and kids," Julio continued. "Those people labored in the fields for chump change and got sprayed with insecticide. Cesar stood up for them. He was sometimes so tired he could hardly stand up, but he knew what he was doing was important. So he worked and he marched and he fasted."

Julio paused for a second to see whether he was getting through to Ernesto. "He cared about the people man. We should all care about the people. We should care about the teenagers in the *barrio* who'd maybe go to college and have a life if the scholarship program came back. We all should care man."

"Come on Julio," Ernesto snapped. "This isn't some great cause like a farm workers strike or something. This is just a city council race, you know? I mean, these guys are just pencil pushers anyway."

"Yeah?" Julio prodded. "Your old man, Mr. Sandoval, he told us something in class the other day. He said he got one of those Sena scholarships when he was a kid. That's the scholarship that old-time councilman Maynard put in place. Maynard pounded the pavements around here getting the businesspeople to contribute money. He got it done. He wasn't pushing no pencils man. He was working for the people. Emilio Ibarra promised to bring that back. Listen up, Ernie. Your own father got a helpin' hand when he needed it. There are kids out there right now who need a hand up too from a councilman who cares."

"I gotta get to English so Ms. Hunt can approve my paper," Ernesto blurted. He rushed ahead of Julio and Abel.

Ernesto was feeling really frustrated. He knew all about Mr. Maynard. He was an icon in the Sandoval family. A photograph of the smiling white-haired man hung on the wall in the den. The picture was there in Los Angeles when the Sandovals lived there. When they moved back to the *barrio*, it came too. Now it hung on the wall in the den in the little house on Wren Street.

"Think about it man," Julio yelled after Ernesto. "You're better than you're lookin' right now, dude. You're *way* better than you're lookin' right now."

Ernesto rushed into Ms. Hunt's classroom only minutes before class was due to begin. He was still a little winded from his sprint.

"Ms. Hunt," Ernesto told her, "I'd like to do my report on F. Scott Fitzgerald. He was an interesting guy. And he kind of represented the era he lived in, the Roaring Twenties. I'm really fascinated by that."

"Good choice, Ernesto," Ms. Hunt said. "I'll write you down for it. I'm looking forward to seeing your report."

Ernesto went to his desk and sat down. Clay Aguirre came in and took his usual place in the back of the classroom. Ernesto glanced back once before class began. Clay aimed his index finger at Ernesto and spoke in a soft voice. "She's wavering, dude. I think you're losing the battle man." Ernesto ignored Clay but knew what he meant. Ernesto took a long, deep breath.

CHAPTER THREE

It was hard for Ernesto to concentrate on Ms. Hunt's class. He kept going over his choices, and all of them were bad. He could join the *Zapatistas* and explain to Naomi that he was doing what his conscience told him. She would respect that. He was sure of it. But eventually word would get back to Felix Martinez, and he'd be outraged. Naomi was already struggling in that family. If Ernesto made an enemy of her father, she would be in even more trouble.

Felix Martinez was an unforgiving man. He had had no contact with his two older sons, Orlando and Manny, since he threw them out of the house three years ago. He even denied his wife contact with them.

Ernesto had secretly arranged for Mrs. Martinez to meet with them at a restaurant a few weeks ago. Mr. Martinez never knew, but the get-together was a huge blessing to Linda Martinez and Naomi. Naomi held out a hope that someday her father would relent and forgive his sons. But Ernesto wasn't sure. Nor was he sure that Felix Martinez would ever forgive *him* if he became a *Zapatista*.

Felix Martinez had the power to make Naomi and Ernesto miserable if he wanted to. And in the midst of it all was Clay Aguirre. He was stalking his prey like a predator and waiting for the opportunity to make his move.

Usually Ernesto could take a problem like this to his father and get some advice. But this time he didn't want to do that. He already knew what Luis Sandoval would say.

"Go with your conscience *mi hijo*," would be Dad's words. "Don't make your decision just to avoid difficulties. Most right choices are difficult. If good people made choices only for what was easy and trouble free, then few people would have the courage to do what was right."

Ernesto figured that would mean joining the *Zapatistas*, and he wasn't ready to do that. He thought he could still walk a tightrope and avoid arousing Felix Martinez's wrath.

Sometimes Ernesto drove home from school, but usually he walked or jogged. Every mile he ran made him stronger for track, and he enjoyed running. It cleared his mind in a way that few things did.

As he ran, Ernesto usually didn't look left or right. He just focused on the run. But this afternoon he noticed a building on Washington Street. It was a neat little white stucco building with a stone monument out front. On the monument was a bronze plate. The American flag flew from the building.

Ernesto stopped, recognizing Veterans Hall. The veterans organization had been at work for fifty years, providing help and fellowship for those returning from many wars—World Wars I and II, Korea, Vietnam, and the wars in the Middle East. When Ernesto was just a small boy living with his parents in Los Angeles, the vets would come down to the *barrio* often to visit his father's parents and siblings. *Abuelo* Luis, Lena's husband, was a veteran of the Vietnam War. That war was just a name in the Chavez students' history books, but it meant a lot to men of *Abuelo* Luis's generation. Ernesto remembered coming to this small building with his father and grandfather for beans, rice, *tortillas, fideo*, and *albóndigas*.

For some reason, Ernesto now looked more closely at the bronze nameplate than he had ever looked before. Listed on it were the names of the locals who had lost their lives in the wars America had fought. A lot of them were Latino. The nameplate had empty spaces at the end. But it was filling up with the names of local men and women from the wars in Iraq and Afghanistan. Some of the names were Latino too.

Ernesto found the name of the first young man who left the *barrio* to fight in Vietnam and did not return alive. Nicolo Sena died in Vietnam in 1968. He was nineteen years old, only three years older than Ernesto was now. Because Nicolo was the first Mexican-American soldier from the area to die in Vietnam, Councilman Maynard named the scholarship in his honor.

Ernesto stood there in the warm autumn air, looking at the name. He pictured Nicolo coming home in one of those caskets draped with the American flag. On the day of his burial, he visualized the pallbearers folding the flag carefully and handing it to his parents. He was born in 1949, and he died in 1968. If he were alive today, Ernesto thought, he would be one of the silver-haired veterans coming here for fellowship. His parents were probably long dead by now, but they would surely have lived long enough to be proud that a scholarship had been named for their son. Ernesto wondered whether Nicolo had brothers or sisters. Did they come here to look at the bronze plate and to remember their brother who never grew old?

Ernesto felt strange standing there and looking at the boy's name. Thinking about a young man he never knew and would never know.

"Anything I can do to help you?" a voice came from behind Ernesto. The man had come up without Ernesto seeing him. The man had white hair and a lined face.

"Uh no, thanks. I was just looking at this—" He didn't know how to describe it.

"Honor roll," the man offered. "It's an honor roll for the war dead. Boys from the *barrio* who died in the wars. We got a young lady's name there now too. She was the first woman from the *barrio* to die in Afghanistan. Marguerite Gutierrez. Right there near the bottom. Died about six months after she got there. IED."

"My dad served in Iraq, but he came home safely. Just a scar," Ernesto commented.

"Anyone special you're looking for, son?" the man asked with a smile.

"Nicolo Sena," Ernesto replied. "I was looking for him, but I found him. He was the first to die in Vietnam. They named that scholarship for him, huh? My dad got to go to college and become a teacher with the help of that scholarship. It made a difference in my family's life. I hope there's somebody from the Sena family still alive to remember Nicolo and, you know, to be proud."

"He was my big brother," the man said. He held out his hand. "I'm Felipe Sena. I'm one of the guys in charge of the post here. I went to Nam too, but I made it home. By the time I went, the casualties were going down. Nicolo died in the Tet Offensive. Young fella like you probably never heard of the Tet Offensive. Long time ago."

Ernesto grasped the man's hand. "I'm Ernesto Sandoval. Like I said, my father, Luis Sandoval, he studied to be a teacher with the scholarship named for your brother. And now he teaches history at Chavez High where I go."

"Is that right?" the man exclaimed. "Well, I'm glad to meet you, Ernesto. There's talk of the scholarship being renewed. That would be a wonderful thing. I don't know if your father belongs to the post here. I don't recollect the name. A lot of the younger men don't belong. Most of the guys we got coming here are silver foxes like me." He chuckled and added, "You tell your father to drop in some night when we're serving chicken *enchiladas* He should bring the whole family."

"I'll tell him, thanks," Ernesto responded, then he jogged on.

Ernesto thought Mr. Sena was a nice guy. Ernesto had no doubt whom the man would be supporting in the upcoming council election. But Ernesto didn't want to think about the election now. He wanted to think of *anything* but that.

That evening, Ernesto got a call on his cell phone. "Hey Ernie, Orlando here." It was Orlando Martinez, Felix's eldest son. He was a singer-musician with the Oscar Perez band in Los Angeles. Three years ago, when Felix Martinez struck his wife, Orlando decked him. The father could not forgive his son for that. He threw him out of the house that night.

"Hey Orlando, how's it going?" Ernesto asked.

"Great," Orlando replied. "We're busy. We did a gig in Frisco, and we got one in Vegas next month." He laughed happily. "Reason I called is, we're coming down to the *barrio* next week to do a benefit concert for Emilio Ibarra's campaign. We'll be performing at Hortencia's tamale place. That'll be next Friday, a week from tomorrow. We hit there in the afternoon, play, and then leave right after the show. You know how hot Oscar is for that chick. Well, she's going all out, opening the patio. She's even using the neighbor's property for the overflow. It'd be great if you could bring Mama and Naomi. Can you sneak them out without my father knowing?"

Ernesto got numb. He didn't respond.

"We gotta get that stooge, Esposito, out of there man," Orlando continued. "Ibarra is a firecracker. He'll do great things for the *barrio*. Esposito been hanging around for almost ten years, and he's like rotten fruit. He needs to go. So what do you think?"

"Orlando, you gotta know that—" Ernesto began to say.

"Yeah, Esposito is my father's cousin," Orlando finished the sentence for Ernesto. "And Dad thinks he's the best thing since guacamole. They're tight as the belt on a fat man. When I was living with my parents, Esposito would come over for dinner a lot. My father idolized him. He was the man. I got a lot of disagreements with my father, but at least he's a hardworking man. This

Esposito don't get out of his chair unless it's to answer the call of nature."

"Your father wouldn't like it if he knew his wife and daughter were at an Ibarra rally, dude," Ernesto advised.

"Yeah," Orlando concurred. "Esposito gets Dad tickets to the playoff football games. When the big shots from Washington come to town, Dad gets to mingle with them because of his cousin. Dad even got his picture taken with the president of the United States once, courtesy of Esposito. I think my father is prouder of that picture than he is of any of us kids in our graduation gowns. Monte Esposito takes care of his cronies, all right. But the rest of the people can go to hell for all he cares."

Ernesto was still silent, feeling the sharp thorns of his dilemma starting to poke him. "We gotta get him out of there man," Orlando went on. "Ibarra, he's just an ordinary working man with a lot of natural savvy. He helped run some of the federal programs in the *barrio* for the local congressman. Ibarra could do a bang-up job for the people. So, listen, check with Mom and Naomi and see what you can do. The concert is next Friday night."

"I'll uh . . . talk to them," Ernesto finally said. He and Orlando talked about the details of the meeting and then ended the call.

Ernesto waited until later in the afternoon that day to bring up the subject with Naomi. That was when Felix Martinez hung out at the pool hall with his friends. As he drove Naomi home from school, he told her about the benefit concert. "Orlando is really excited about it, and he'd love for you and your mom to come," Ernesto concluded.

"Ohhhh," Naomi sighed. "Mom would be so happy to see Orlando again. The last time she got to see him, she didn't stop talking to me about it for days. I would love to see my brother too and to see him perform with the band. That would be so cool."

"Naomi," Ernesto suggested, "on Friday night we could do what we did before. Remember? You and your mom met Orlando and Manny at the restaurant. We could say you were going to see her sister."

Naomi frowned. "Oh Ernie, everybody from the *barrio* will be there. It'd get back to Dad that we were at the *Zapatista* concert for Mr. Ibarra. That would be such a betrayal in Dad's mind. I mean, his own wife and daughter at a fund-raiser for a guy who's trying to unseat his cousin Monte. The dinner that time was different. It was secret, and nobody saw us."

"Naomi, this whole thing is making me sick," Ernesto confessed in frustration. "Things don't have to be this way. That governor California had, the guy from Austria, the action hero. He was a big Republican, and his wife was a Democrat. And they got along fine. I mean it's only politics, stupid politics. Your mom and you too, you both deserve to see your family."

Naomi gave Ernesto a dark look. "Ernie, it's easy for you to say. You don't have to live with my dad. He and Monte have been friends since first grade. Mom told me they'd tear around the *barrio* together in a hot rod they built. Dad's closer to him than almost anybody. When he got on the city council, Dad went nuts with pride. He's Dad's claim to fame. I guess. I mean, my father hasn't got much to brag about. But he's the cousin of Councilman Monte Esposito. That's big stuff."

"Well, let's talk to your mom at least," Ernesto suggested as they neared the house on Bluebird Street.

Ernesto and Naomi went in the house and told Linda Martinez that Orlando was coming to town next Friday night. She lit up like a Christmas tree. She clamped her hands to her cheeks, and her face turned rosy. "Oh! *Mi hijo*! I miss him so much. *El primogénito*! How happy I was when he came into the world. How I would love to see him!"

"Mom," Naomi explained, "Orlando is performing with the Oscar Perez band at Hortencia's a week from tomorrow. But it's a benefit for Emilio Ibarra's campaign. It's a fund-raiser for him. Orlando is coming in the afternoon, and he's returning with the band that night."

A look of disappointment and anguish took the joy from Linda Martinez's face. Her eyes turned fearful. Like a dark, frightening beast, the fear crawled through her eyes, dimming their brightness and anticipation. "Oh, Felix would be outraged if Naomi and I went to a fund-raiser for Mr. Ibarra. He hates Emilio Ibarra. He thunders around the house cursing the man as an upstart who wants to take power from his wonderful cousin."

Mrs. Martinez stared past her daughter and Ernesto. She seemed to be weighing the consequences of seeing her son. "If we went to the concert," she declared, "it would be like stabbing Felix in the back. He'd be so angry. I cannot even imagine it. And he *would* find out because of all the people there. Someone would tell him." Tears sparkled in the woman's eyes. "Oh, but I would so love to see my son. It breaks my heart that he will be here in the *barrio* and I cannot see him."

Ernesto felt really sorry for Naomi's mother. It made him so angry that this good woman had to live in fear of her husband. But he could do nothing to help her. Still, Ernesto searched his mind for a solution to this specific problem.

"I'll tell you what, Mrs. Martinez," Ernesto suggested. "I'll call Orlando and find out when he's getting into town. Maybe he'd have a little time to meet us somewhere private before he goes to Hortencia's. Like maybe we can grab twenty minutes and go with him to get coffee or something. Just the four of us. I'm sure Orlando would go along with that. He wants to see you guys as much as you want to see him. He misses his family."

Mrs. Martinez smiled. "Oh Ernie, you are just the sweetest boy. Maria can be so proud of you. Maria and your father have raised a good son, one with a compassionate heart."

"I'll see what I can do," Ernesto promised.

Mrs. Martinez went into the kitchen to
start dinner. Ernesto and Naomi went into
the backyard of the Martinez home and sat
on the stone bench. Ernesto looked at the
cute little elves cavorting in the whimsical
garden and sitting on plastic mushrooms.
Naomi told him that her father had designed
this lovely place. That such a harsh man had
this side to his nature seemed impossible.

"That was so incredibly thoughtful of
you, Ernie," Naomi said. "Trying to arrange
a way for us to meet with my brother. I just
can't get over how nice you are."

"Oh, don't go overboard," Ernesto
protested. "I just feel so sorry for your
mom. And you too. Orlando and Manny are
good guys. It's not fair that the family has
to be kept apart like this. Your father makes
such a big deal about his friendship with his
cousin. But what about his own boys?"

"I know," Naomi agreed sadly. "It
would be great if our stupid hearts didn't

get involved. If only we could just be totally logical, sort of like that guy who was in the Star Trek movies—Spock. I mean, logically, I know that my dad is mean and unreasonable. I know that Mom should have taken us and left him a long time ago. And I know now we should go off by ourselves, Mom and me and Zack. We should just let Dad stew in his own juice. We'd all get along fine. Orlando and Manny could hang with us anytime. And it'd be all good. No more dark secrets. No more worrying about Dad exploding in one of his rages when he finds something out."

Naomi stared at the elves for a few seconds. "But the thought of my father, abandoned, rejected. No family, I just can't deal with it. It tears me apart. Mom can't do it either. We love him. He's taken care of us all these years, and we . . . love him. Our lousy, stupid hearts get in the way."

Ernesto put his arms around Naomi's shoulders. "No, don't say that. You're talking about the best part of being human—

having a heart, having compassion. If we just operated on logic, we'd be computers. Who wants to be a computer?"

"The terrible part of it is," Naomi went on, "I don't think it will ever end. I had an uncle once, Uncle Leon. He was dad's brother, and he was just like Dad. He was estranged from half his family too. I remember when Uncle Leon was dying. He wouldn't let his oldest daughter into the room at all. She stood crying out in the hall at the hospital. She'd defied her father. She married a boy he didn't approve of, and he cut her off."

Naomi shook her head in exasperation. "Everybody tried to reconcile them when Uncle Leon was dying. Padre Benito tried, and even some of the nurses tried. But Uncle Leon would never forgive his daughter. I'll never forget being in the hospital with my parents. I was fourteen. My cousin was screaming when her father died without forgiving her. She was sure they would have one moment together before . . ."

Tears welled in Naomi's eyes from the memory. "She kept screaming 'Daddy! Daddy! Daddy!' Oh Ernie, love is supposed to be the strongest emotion. But sometimes hate is stronger than love."

Ernesto gently pulled her against him, and she lay her head on his shoulder.

CHAPTER FOUR

Oh man!" Orlando growled when Ernesto called him Saturday morning. "This is almost too much. The old *diablo* strikes again."

"I hear you, dude," Ernesto sympathized. "But your mom and Naomi really want to see you. You shoulda seen your mom's face when I told her you'd be in town. Maybe you could see your way clear to just carve out a little time for us to meet you somewhere near Hortencia's. You could just, you know, spend a little time with Naomi and your mom. It'd mean the world to them."

"Ernesto Sandoval, you know what?" Orlando declared. "You told me once you thought you'd be a teacher like your dad. Scratch that, man. You need to be a politician. You can twist a guy's arm and get him to do anything. That's a talent a politician really needs to get things done. You're something else, Ernie. Okay, you win. We're due in around six on Friday, and the benefit starts at eight. I'll ask Oscar to drop me from the bus at . . . how about La Abeja? That still in business?"

"Yeah, it is," Ernesto replied. "That'd be perfect."

"Okay, meet me there," Orlando directed. "Then, after we grab a bite, you can drive me over to Hortencia's. Then we're back to business. Is that good?"

"Great, man," Ernesto said. "I'll be there with Naomi and your mom."

"You're a good guy, Ernie," Orlando told him. "A real good guy. I'm glad you and my sister are hanging out."

Next, Ernesto called Naomi and described the arrangement.

"Ernie!" she cried. He could see her smiling at the other end of the line. He could see her. He was only a few blocks from her house, and he could feel her joy.

Right after school on the next Friday, Naomi climbed into Ernesto's Volvo, and they drove home to get her mother.

As they got out of the car, Ernesto saw Brutus and tossed a ball for him. Then he went in the Martinez house. Felix was sitting in front of the television set, cursing at a newscaster for putting the wrong spin on something.

"You're full of it, lady!" he yelled, grabbing the remote and changing the station.

"Well, Felix," Linda Martinez told him, "Ernie is driving me over to see my sister now. I should be home around seven, seven thirty. I made dinner. You just need to reheat it."

"Yeah, okay!" Felix Martinez snarled. "It tastes so bad, it don't matter if it's hot or cold anyway."

Ernesto winced. But Mrs. Martinez was just happy to be going to see her son. The slur on her cooking didn't even hurt.

Ernesto parked at La Abeja. Orlando had said to look for a big red and green bus carrying the Oscar Perez band. It would be turning at the intersection at the corner where the restaurant was. Sure enough, the bus came into view, and Orlando hopped down from it. He trotted toward the Volvo, where Ernesto waited with Mrs. Martinez and Naomi.

Mrs. Martinez couldn't restrain herself. She jumped from the car and ran to meet her son. As she sprinted toward the handsome young man, she didn't seem like a woman in her late forties. She seemed like a teenager.

Orlando took his mother in his arms. From a distance, they looked like a big man embracing a child. She was so small in comparison to her son. Like his father, Orlando was well over six feet tall, whereas his mother was barely five feet two inches.

Naomi caught up to them, and Orlando hugged his sister too. The three of them walked together into La Abeja. They chattered happily as Ernesto brought up the rear.

When they were seated, Mrs. Martinez looked lovingly at her son. "Oh Orlando, you look so wonderful, so handsome!" Linda Martinez gushed. "*Mi hijo*! *Mi hijo*!" Then she said, "How is Manny? Is Manny doing better?"

"Yeah, Mama," Orlando assured her. "He had to stay in LA to work on the equipment for our Vegas gig. But he'll be coming down to the *barrio* pretty soon. He's put on a lot of weight since he's eating regular again. He told me to give you his love."

The son leaned back in his chair and looked directly at his mother. "So Mama, he hasn't changed, huh?"

Linda Martinez's smile faded. "You mean, your father?" she asked.

"Yeah, who else?" Orlando replied with disgust.

"He doesn't change, Orlando," Mrs. Martinez answered sadly, nodding her head. "Right now he's very upset that Mr. Ibarra is challenging his cousin, Monte Esposito, for the city council. Last time Monte ran, there was no opposition. It looked like he had everything wrapped up this time too, but they found a candidate with the courage to challenge him. Monte has some friends with bad character. Many people didn't want to cross him. But Emilio Ibarra is a very courageous man. And when Monte went to the Bahamas and spent so much money, people were angry. They got fed up."

"It's about time the bum is kicked out," Orlando stated hotly. "Ibarra is a great candidate. He cares about people. He's always involved in stuff like the Thanksgiving baskets and Christmas presents for the poor kids. We haven't had a good person in that council seat since Mr. Maynard, years ago."

They ordered chicken burritos and Mayan hot chocolates. Orlando looked at his mother and asked, "Mama, do you have any fun? I would like to take you somewhere where you could have a real vacation, like maybe to Hawaii. Where would you like to go, Mama? I have some money now, and I will pay for everything."

Linda Martinez looked wistful. Orlando may as well have been asking her to visit a distant planet in another galaxy. There was as good a chance of going to outer space as going anywhere. She could not leave her husband and go somewhere for even a week. Felix Martinez didn't believe in vacations.

Still, Orlando's offer brought a look of almost forlorn delight to the woman's face, as if just fantasizing about a trip was enjoyable. She imagined herself boarding a plane for Hawaii and getting off on a tropical island. Then someone would put a fragrant lei her shoulders in welcome. But going anywhere was out of the question. A trip would never happen.

Linda Martinez forced a smile to her lips and spoke to her son. "It is so sweet of you to offer me a vacation, Orlando. But I have a good life. I have a nice home and some wonderful friends at church. We sometimes go to breakfast after mass. I enjoy watching movies on television. We have a nice big television set now. I rent a lot of movies too. I like the older ones that came out when I was young."

"Well Mama, maybe sometime . . . maybe sometime I can take you to Hawaii," Orlando said resignedly.

When they finished their meal, Ernesto took Orlando to Hortencia's, where a big crowd was gathering. The Perez bus was already parked there, and red, white, and blue balloons were everywhere. Ernesto could hear the music as the band was tuning up. Orlando, sitting in the front seat with Ernesto, turned to him and stuck out his hand.

"Thanks for making my visit with Mom and Naomi happen, dude," he told Ernesto, shaking hands. Then, turning to the back seat, he said, "Bye Mama! Bye little sister!" He hopped out and ran into Hortencia's to join the concert.

Ernesto drove Naomi and her mother home. He would have loved to stay at Hortencia's with Naomi and enjoy the evening. He always liked being around *Tía* Hortencia. He wished they could all have stayed for the music and the good food and the fun. But it couldn't be.

When Ernesto got home, Katalina and Juanita were getting ready for bed. *Abuela* was sitting in the living room, knitting.

"Hello Ernesto," *Abuela* greeted him. "Your mama and papa went to Hortencia's for the benefit concert. They said they'd be home around ten thirty or eleven." Ernesto knew Mom and Dad were going to the concert. They didn't talk much about it because they knew the election was a problem area for Ernesto. Luis Sandoval had been a close friend of Emilio Ibarra since they both were boys. They played together in Little League. They were both boy scouts. There was never a question about Ernesto's father supporting Ibarra's candidacy.

Ernesto sat down in the living room and confided in his grandmother. "*Abuela*, you know I'm going with Naomi Martinez. Her father is the cousin of Councilman Esposito."

The older woman nodded. "I know, Ernesto. It makes it hard for Naomi and for you. Naomi is such a nice girl. I remember when she was born. Such a beautiful child. Their first daughter. The other three were sons. Linda was afraid she would never have a daughter. I used to see Linda in church with little Naomi in her pink ribbons and fluffy dresses. Like a little doll. Linda was so happy to have her little *niña*. When Naomi made her first communion, she looked like an angel in her white veil and dress." *Abuela* continued to knit but smiled at the memory.

Ernesto smiled too. He was with his family in Los Angeles when Naomi was a little girl growing up in the *barrio*. He was barely six when they moved, and he had no memories of the Martinez family. But, considering what Naomi looked like now, Ernesto could imagine what a lovely child she must have been.

Abuela held up the portion of the little sweater that was finished. She looked at it approvingly.

"You make such beautiful stuff," Ernesto commented.

Abuela was still thinking of the Martinez family, and she looked serious. "I remember when Felix and Linda were young parents, Ernesto. Even then Felix was the ruler of the house. It was not that way in my house. Your grandfather was a strong man, but I was a strong woman too. We decided on things together. My husband was proud of me for being strong. 'I do not want a servant,' he said. 'I want a partner.' And that is what we were—partners. We had five children, and it was a struggle. We had to both be strong. I think that's better. Luis and your mama are like that too. All our children were raised to be strong, the girls as well as the boys."

"Mrs. Martinez is afraid of her husband," Ernesto said. He was nervously weaving his fingers in and out of each other in his lap. He loved Naomi with all his heart, but the situation in her home bothered him. It was like a dark cloud hanging over everything, waiting to grow even darker and explode with thunder and rain.

"I know," *Abuela* agreed, shaking her head softly.

Ernesto felt uncomfortable discussing the topic further with his grandmother. So he let out a big yawn. "*Abuela*, I think Katalina and Juanita have the right idea about getting to bed. It's been such a long week."

"Okay, *mi hijo*, but if you need to talk more, I am here to listen," she said.

When Maria and Luis Sandoval came home at eleven o'clock, Ernesto had gone to bed but was awake. *Abuela* was still knitting in the living room. She had insomnia sometimes, and she knitted into the night—knitted and prayed. Ernesto heard his father's voice, filled with excitement. "It was wonderful, Mama. Such a big crowd. I've never seen people in the *barrio* so excited about a local race. Emilio was there for most of the evening. That big, booming voice, that big laugh. He danced with Conchita, and he danced with Carmen."

"He danced with me too, Mama," Maria Sandoval giggled.

"I wished Ernie could have been there," Dad said. "I know he would have gotten a big kick out of it."

"Julio Avila and his father were there," Dad added. "Julio and the kids in the *Zapatista* club are anxious to help. They said they'd make telephone calls and get out there going door to door for Emilio."

Ernesto lay in bed, wide awake. The *barrio* needed Emilio Zapata Ibarra. The campaign was like a wonderful parade getting underway. Drums were pounding, and horns were tooting. Excited, dedicated people were setting out to change the world, at least this part of the world. And Ernesto refused to march.

As Ernesto drifted off to sleep, his thoughts were about how the barrio needed a new leader. Emilio Ibarra was old enough to understand the local problems. And he was young enough to have the energy and enthusiasm to solve them. He was about the same age as Ernesto's father. Monte Esposito was in his midfifties, and he looked much older. He was a heavyset man, and his body language conveyed weariness and boredom. He might have had some good ideas when he was elected ten years ago. But he never implemented them. Now he probably didn't even care about them anymore.

When Ernesto got to school on Monday, the first person he saw was Naomi. She had biked in. And she looked as though she had been crying. Ernesto rushed over to her and asked, "What's the matter? You okay?"

"Yeah, I'm okay," Naomi replied, locking her bike in the rack. "But last night at our house was so awful. One of Dad's drinking buddies saw the big crowd at Hortencia's on Friday. So he went over to investigate. He recognized Orlando performing. He knew it was my dad's son. This guy, he couldn't wait to call Dad up. He just had to let him know his son was at a campaign rally for Emilio Ibarra. This guy, he really enjoyed rubbing it in. Dad went ballistic."

"Oh man!" Ernesto groaned, as they walked slowly toward their first class.

"Yeah," Naomi went on, "Dad was raging around the house like a wild bull. He was saying such terrible things about Orlando. Oh Ernie, I've been hoping that, little by little, Dad might soften up on Orlando and Manny. Maybe our family could be healed. But now it's worse than ever. Dad was saying Orlando is a traitor to the family. He better never show his face around the Martinez house. He'll get the thrashing of his life. Then poor Mom started crying, and that made Dad even madder."

Naomi shook her head. "Then Dad starts in on Mom, saying she's weak and she's an idiot. If she hadn't coddled Orlando and Manny, they wouldn't have grown up to be such creeps. He said it was all her fault. The boys went bad because she was too easy on them. He started bringing up every little thing Orlando did. He should've been whipped because he stole a peach from the open air market. But, no, Mom wouldn't let Dad whip him . . ."

"I'm sorry, Naomi," Ernesto sympathized. "It must have been hard on you."

"Dad said he's going to work really hard on his cousin's campaign now to make sure Ibarra loses," Naomi went on. "He ordered me and Zack. We've got to pass out flyers and go door to door, telling people why they should reelect Esposito. We're supposed to tell everybody what a rotten person Mr. Ibarra is. By this time, Dad's breathing so hard, I'm afraid he's going to have a heart attack. He's telling me and Zack that we're his only loyal kids left. We have to do double duty to make up for those traitors, Orlando and Manny."

Naomi was staring straight ahead as she walked, her books clutched in front of her. "Zack said he'd do it. You know Zack. He'll do anything to please Dad. But I just can't. I didn't tell him I can't, not in the mood he was in. But the thing is, I don't think Esposito is any good. I think Mr. Ibarra would be good for the *barrio*. I can stay out of the whole thing, even though I'd like to help Ibarra. But no way am I going to work for Esposito. No way."

Ernesto sighed deeply. He didn't know what to say. Then he remembered something his friend, Abel Ruiz, had shared with him. He started telling Naomi Abel's story. "Abel, he's got this really smart brother, Tomás. For years now, Abel's parents have been saying Tomás is the smart one, and Abel is the dumb loser. Well, Abel always got along with his dad 'cause he's kinda weak, and he doesn't say much. But Abel's mom is real strong. She kinda always discouraged Abel from trying anything because she said he'd just screw it up."

Ernesto glanced at Naomi, to make sure she was listening. She was. "Abel was really cowed by her attitude. It got so he didn't have the courage to do anything. But then one day he just stood up to her. He wanted to do something she was dead set against. She like told him, 'You are not doing it.' And Abel goes, 'I'm doing it, and you can't stop me. That's the way it is.' Well, Abel figured the whole world might flip upside down in that moment. That's because he'd never stood up to his mom like that before. But Abel's strong, domineering mom backed down. Now things are much better for Abel."

Ernesto then said what he'd been leading up to. He stopped walking and turned to Naomi, who now faced him. "So, Naomi, if push comes to shove, you need to tell your father how you feel in a calm, respectful way. You got to let him know you're not working on Esposito's campaign because you don't believe in it. And that's that."

Naomi's eyes became very wide, and she stared at Ernesto. "I've never stood up to him like that," she said.

"Naomi, he loves you," Ernesto assured her. "You're his daughter, and he loves you. He hasn't ever hit you or anything, has he?"

"Oh no, never," Naomi responded. "We've always gotten along good. But I've never defied him before, not in a big way. When we got Brutus—the pit bull—I knew it would drive Mom crazy. I felt so sorry for Mom because she lived in terror of that dog. I knew I should go to my father. I knew I should demand he get rid of the dog and get a nice little dog that Mom wouldn't be afraid of. But I never did. I watched Mom suffer in terror, and I just kept my mouth shut. I was ashamed of myself for that. It all turned out okay in the end, sure. And Brutus turned out to be a nice dog. Now Mom likes him too. But still I was a coward or I would have stood by Mom."

"Naomi, that was then. This is now." Ernesto said. "You can do it. You can be very quiet and very firm. Don't get mad. You don't have to remind your father of all the creepy things he's done to keep the family in line. You don't have to say that you're a *Zapatista*. You don't have to say that you'll be running around the neigh borhood handing out flyers for Emilio. You don't have to go that far. That would be too much for him to swallow. But just tell him that you are not getting involved in Esposito's campaign, not now, not *ever*."

"I don't know," Naomi objected. "Like I say, I've never stood up to him before. *I want to*. It's like when I was with Clay. Sometimes he was so rude, he made me mad. He'd yell at me for some silly thing, and I'd stand there and take it. I'd feel like a fool, but I wouldn't stand up to him."

Ernesto took hold of Naomi's shoulders and looked directly into her amazing violet eyes. "Babe, you *did* stand up to Clay. A lot of girls and women out there have been hit by a boyfriend, and they made up with the guy afterward. But you didn't. You had the courage to end it. I know you cared a lot for Clay. There had to have been times when you wanted to forgive him and get back with him. But you stuck to your guns. You knew what he did was wrong. and you didn't want any part of it anymore."

Ernesto waited a couple of seconds to let his words sink in. Then he spoke again. "That took a lot of courage. I was so proud of you, Naomi. Yeah, I wanted for us to get together. But even if that had never happened, I would have still been proud of you for what you did. You can stand up to your father too. You can be respectful to him and still stand up to him. Just tell him that you love him, but you are not campaigning for Esposito . . ."

"I guess I could try," Naomi acceded.

"No, don't say that," Ernesto commanded. "When people say they'll try to do something, they end up not doing it."

The morning was cool, and Ernesto was wearing a hoodie. When he embraced Naomi, she was lost in his arms, and the two of them looked like one.

CHAPTER FIVE

When Ernesto went to work at the pizzeria that afternoon, he heard his boss, Bashar, talking to a customer. "Ycah, I'm gonna be an American citizen next year. I wish I was one right now so I could vote for that guy Emilio Ibarra. I wanna get that lousy Esposito out of there. He voted to raise business licenses on all the little merchants and not the big guys. That's 'cause the big guys are putting money in his pocket."

Ernesto slipped on his T-shirt with the words "Best Pizza" on the back. He tried to ignore the conversation, but Bashar had a very loud voice.

"We got businesses closing down all over the place," Bashar complained. "Taco stand went down, the chicken place. We don't need a kick in the pants from those lousy politicians."

The customer took his pizza and left. Then Bashar turned to Ernesto, a big grin on his face. "You're one of those *Zapatistas,* right? Seems like all the kids at Chavez are for the big guy with the mustache."

"I go to school with Mr. Ibarra's daughter, Carmen," Ernesto answered, trying to evade the question. "We're really good friends. I like Emilio Ibarra. Seems like a good man, but I'm not too involved in the campaign. I guess the best man will win. The best man usually wins."

Bashar frowned. He was usually smiling, but he wasn't smiling now. "Best one don't always win, kid," he growled. "Sometimes the worst one wins. Sometimes people don't care enough to roll up their sleeves and work for the good candidates. Then, well, the crooks come marching in, see?"

"Yeah, yeah, you're right," Ernesto agreed, glad to wiggle off the hook when a flurry of customers came in.

Mira Nuñez, the girl Clay dated in a vain effort to make Naomi jealous, came in with two girlfriends. Ernesto didn't know Mira well, but she was in Ms. Hunt's class. Once, when she was out sick, Ernesto made a copy of his class notes for her. He often did the same for students out sick. Missing a class could really make a difference at test time. After Ernesto did her that favor, Mira always greeted him with a smile and a cheery hello. Ernesto could see Mira was stuck on Clay, but he wasn't showing her much attention.

"Hi Ernie," Mira greeted him. "I guess we'll have salads. We're on a diet." The other two girls giggled. None of the three had a weight problem. But they all wanted to look sensational in skinny jeans.

Mira had a big stack of political flyers in her purse. Ernesto noticed they were for Monte Esposito.

"Clay is after me to pass these out," Mira remarked. "You want one, Ernie? It's about the election. The fat guy in the picture on the flyer, I guess he's running. I don't know what it's all about. But I'm Clay Aguirre's girlfriend, and he really wants me to spread these around."

Ernesto took one of the flyers and stuffed it in the wastebasket when Mira wasn't looking. He didn't want to tell Mira why Clay was working so hard for Monte Esposito. Clay just wanted to gain brownie points with Naomi's father. He hoped that Felix Martinez would help him win Naomi back. It was a futile effort, but Clay was desperate. He really wanted Naomi back. He bitterly regretted that fierce argument when he lost his temper so badly that he actually punched Naomi. He wanted to kick himself from one end of the *barrio* to the other for doing that. He had been dating the most beautiful girl at Chavez, and he blew it all.

One of the girls with Mira made a comment. "Most of my friends at school don't want this fat guy. They want the dude with the big mustache. They call themselves *Zapatistas*, and I think that's cool." The girl laughed then and added, "I guess this Ibarra guy is named for some old dude who used to live in Mexico. I don't know who he was. I usually get my beauty sleep in history."

"Emiliano Zapata was a revolutionary in Mexico around 1911," Ernesto told her. "When I was a sophomore in high school in Los Angeles, we had a class in Mexican history. It was interesting."

"What was he revolting against?" Mira asked.

"There were a few rich guys who owned the sugar plantations down there," Ernesto explained. "And the ordinary people worked like dogs without making much. Zapata wanted the plantations to be divided up among the workers who lived there."

"Boy, Ernie," Mira remarked, "you're smart. You know, the only time I ever had good notes in Ms. Hunt's English class was when you gave me copies of yours. So, did the sugar plantations get busted up and go to the poor?"

"No," Ernesto replied. "This guy Zapata was lured into a trap and executed by the people in power. But many years later, some of his ideas for reform were approved in Mexico."

"See," Mira said. "The in crowd always wins. That's what I told Clay. He doesn't have to be worried that this fat guy won't win. He's in the job now, and he'll be reelected. My mom always votes for the one who's already in there. I wish Clay wasn't so busy with this stupid election. He used to take me out once in a while. Now all he thinks about is getting this fat guy back in office."

Ernesto kept busy with the customers for the next half hour. Then Clay Aguirre appeared with Zack Martinez. When Clay spotted Mira, he called out to her, "Mira, did you pass out all the flyers I gave you?"

"Uh, not yet, Clay, but I'm going to," Mira answered.

Clay walked over to where Mira was sitting and looked in her purse. It was bulging with the flyers. "You didn't pass *any* out. Mira, they're all still here, and you're sitting here feeding your face. What's the matter with you? I ask you to do me a favor, and what happens?"

Ernesto remembered when he first came to Chavez High a few months ago, when Clay and Naomi were still dating. Clay routinely talked to Naomi as he was now talking to Mira. Once, Naomi had forgotten to bring a report to school—one she did for Clay. He yelled at her and called her names in front of the whole class. Ernesto remembered thinking, "Why does that beautiful girl take that from a jerk?"

"I'm sorry, Clay," Mira apologized contritely. "I was just having a little salad here. Then I'll get going with the flyers."

Ernesto glanced at Clay with disgust. He *was* very good-looking, with a great build and big shoulders. But he was so self-centered and rude. Ernesto was amazed that so many girls wanted to date him.

"See that you pass them all out, Mira," Clay ordered her. "I don't care how long it takes you. This is very important. We gotta make sure that freak Emilio Ibarra doesn't get on the city council."

In the meantime, Yvette Ozono had come in. She was eating a pizza with a boy from Chavez. Yvette had dropped out of school and had been dating a gangbanger. Then she dropped the punk and found a nice boyfriend, Tommy Alvarado. The gangbanger retaliated by killing Tommy. Yvette went into a deep depression, but Luis Sandoval, with Ernesto's help, rescued her and got her back in school. Now Yvette was a top student in Mr. Cabral's math class. Her whole life had been turned around. One of her best friends at Chavez now was Carmen Ibarra.

She overheard Clay's remark and told him very loudly, "You're all wrong, Clay. Mr. Ibarra isn't a freak. He'll do a great job if he gets on the city council. Esposito is no good. He doesn't help anybody. He doesn't do anything for the kids or the old people or anybody."

Clay sneered in Yvette's direction. He turned to Mira and ordered, "Don't pay any attention to that chick. She's a gang-banger's squeeze. She's living over on Starling with all the dopesters."

"Knock it off, Clay," Ernesto snapped. "You're way out of line."

"Mind your own business, Sandoval," Clay snarled. "Lot of us at Chavez ain't too happy with what your old man is doing. He walks around the streets to get gangbangers back into school. We don't want those punks around. They dropped out, and that should be the end of them."

Alarmed by the loud voices in his pizzeria, Bashar emerged from the kitchen. He looked at Ernesto and asked, "What's going on here? I don't want no fights in my place. If anybody's got a beef, take it outside."

"It's okay," Ernesto assured him. "It's cool."

He smiled over at Yvette and said, "Hey Yvette, I hear you're in the geek squad in Cabral's class. That's pretty cool. You guys are headed for a math competition up in LA next month, right?"

Yvette had looked deeply hurt by Clay's attack, but now her smile had returned. "Yeah. Mr. Cabral is taking four of us. I'm real excited. I've never been in anything like that."

Clay had returned his attention to Mira. "You gonna be grazing on that salad all night? Get a move on, girl. It's late. You gotta pass out all those flyers. Me and Zack are taking Cardinal Street, and you can do Bluebird. Now go!" Clay gave the girl a push that almost knocked her off the stool. The girls with Mira gave her funny looks and rolled their eyes.

Clay, Zack, and Mira rushed out the door. As they did, one of the girls who came in with Mira said to her companion,

"Aguirre isn't *that* cute. If some jock treated me like that, I'd empty the bowl of salsa over his head."

"Here, here!" Ernesto declared.

Bashar stood there for a few seconds, and then he said, "I wish that guy wouldn't come in here. I don't like him. Guys like him always stirring up trouble. They got no respect for other people."

Ernesto had planned to go to Naomi's house when he got off work at eight and pick her up. Then the two of them would hang out for a while. Ernesto was worried about Naomi. He wondered whether she had done what he suggested. Had she told her father she wasn't going to campaign for his cousin? Ernesto was having second thoughts about his advice. Maybe he should have kept his mouth shut. Maybe Naomi had gotten into big trouble with her father.

Ernesto drove up to the Martinez house about ten after eight. Even though it was dark, Zack was in the front yard playing with Brutus.

"Hi Zack," Ernesto said. "Me and Naomi were gonna hang out for a little while."

Brutus ran up to Ernesto, his tail wagging. He waited until Ernesto scratched his head. He liked that.

"Uh, I don't think so," Zack replied.

Ernesto turned cold. "Why? What's the matter?" he asked.

"They're, you know, arguing in there, Mom and Dad," Zack explained. He looked embarrassed. He wasn't strong like Orlando. He wasn't even as strong as Manny. Zack was the weakest of the three boys, the most easily manipulated by his father.

"Where's Naomi?" Ernesto asked. His heart started to pound. He was having even more serious doubts about his advice to her. Maybe Felix Martinez had taken it badly. He was a tough, unpredictable man. He had on a few occasions hit his wife. He had never struck Naomi, but there was always a first time. In the past, Naomi pretty much went along with her father. Maybe his daughter's standing up to him triggered a terrible response.

Zack shrugged and said, "Naomi, she and Dad sorta argued, and Dad's going, 'Even my own daughter—my little girl—is turning on me. If a man can't even rely on his family, his own flesh and blood, then what's he got?'"

"Naomi is okay, right?" Ernesto asked desperately. "I'd like to see her, talk to her. Okay?"

"She's all right," Zack answered, "but, you know, Dad started in blaming Mom like he always does. Blames her for raising us too soft. For coddling Naomi. For not teaching her that a kid has to do what her father says. You know, she needs to do what *he* thinks is best, and it don't matter what she thinks. Dad's saying he's the head of the family. If he wants us all to campaign for his cousin, we gotta do it, no questions asked."

The front door banged open, and Felix Martinez stepped out. He looked at Ernesto with a lot of anger. His eyes looked as though they were smoking. "You're probably behind all this, Ernie. You and that wimpy bleeding heart father of yours. You want Ibarra in there 'cause he'll spend the tax money of hardworking guys like me. And for what? To help a lot of lazy losers who're laying around waitin' for a handout. Naomi never had no crazy ideas like she has now before she met you. All of a sudden, she ain't even willing to help a relative get elected. She ain't loyal to her own blood no more. What's that about?" Mr. Martinez fell silent, glowering at Ernesto.

"Mr. Martinez," Ernesto answered carefully. "Me and Naomi don't talk politics. I think she just wants to concentrate on her schoolwork and not spend a lot of time passing out flyers and stuff like that. I feel like that too. Me and Naomi, we're doing good in school, but we have to work hard. We're not geniuses."

"You're against Monte, aren't you, boy?" Felix Martinez pressed him. "Own up to it, boy."

"I'm not into this business," Ernesto replied.

"My lousy son, Orlando," Mr. Martinez, "he come down from Los Angeles to the *barrio*. And he did a benefit concert for Ibarra. I ain't seen Orlando in three years, not since he raised his hand against me, against his own father. He come down here to help Ibarra, but he don't even bother to see his own family. It's bad enough I got two rotten sons. But now Naomi, she's turning against me too. If a man don't have his own family behind him, then he might as well cash in his chips."

The front door opened again. Naomi stepped out and stood beside her father. "Daddy, I haven't turned against you," she insisted. "I love you very much, and I always will. How many times do I have to explain it? I just don't want to get into the campaign. Politics makes enemies out of friends. I hate it."

"You know what, Naomi?" her father declared. "I gotta give that Clay Aguirre a lot of credit. He comes around here like a man, and he offers to pass out campaign flyers for my cousin. The kid isn't even related to me. And he's more of a son to me than my own two sons, Orlando and Manny."

The man's head swiveled to Ernesto and back to Naomi. "Maybe you made a mistake, Naomi. Maybe you shoulda stuck with Clay. Ernesto here, he's too weak to have any principles. He don't want to get his hands dirty doing precinct work. He's too wishy-washy. I told you a long time ago that Ernie was a wimp, Naomi. Now he's making you weak too. Maybe you shoulda stuck with Aguirre."

Naomi stepped a little closer to her father. "I used to be weak, Dad," she stated. "I was so weak that I let Clay insult me and call me names all those years. Then I got stronger, and I decided I deserved a little respect. And now I'm even stronger. Last year I would have taken those flyers and run all over town with them just 'cause you said so. I would have done it just to please you, Dad, even though I would've hated it."

Mr. Martinez must have been stunned into silence, Ernesto thought. Naomi continued. "I love you, Dad, but I'm strong enough now to say no. You just can't totally control me anymore. Nobody can. It's called courage, Dad. It's not only men who have to have courage. Maybe women need to have it even more than men."

Naomi looked at Ernesto. "We were gonna hang for a while, weren't we, Ernie? Let's go."

Ernesto said nothing as they walked to the car together. He opened the door for her, and she got in. She suggested, "Let's go to Hortencia's and have a *tamale*. I feel like one of Hortencia's *tamales*. I've eaten a lot of *tamales*, but nobody makes them like she does."

"Sounds good," Ernesto agreed. When they were driving toward Hortencia's, Ernesto said, "You're awesome, girl."

Naomi smiled. "That means you didn't hear my knees knocking together. You didn't hear my heart going ninety miles an hour."

Ernesto laughed. "It's okay to have your knees knocking, Naomi, just as long as you don't cave in. And you didn't. I know that was so hard for you to do."

They pulled into the parking lot at Hortencia's. Ernesto was bursting with pride in Naomi.

CHAPTER SIX

Emilio Zapata Ibarra picked up his daughter, Carmen, from school on Tuesday. Usually she walked or biked home. But today her dad pulled up in his own Oldsmobile, which he parked alongside Ernesto's Volvo in the Chavez parking lot.

"Aren't we sporty dudes?" Mr. Ibarra shouted to Ernesto, who was a bit intimidated by Mr. Ibarra. Once he had attended a party at his house, and it was a lot of fun. But the big man with the mustache and the loud voice had made him nervous. Ernesto had seen very little of Mr. Ibarra since the city council race started.

No doubt Carmen had told her father that Ernesto was not actively supporting his campaign because his girlfriend was related to Ibarra's opponent. So now he felt even more uncomfortable meeting him face to face. Ernesto wasn't quite sure how Mr. Ibarra would react. Ernesto didn't actually think he would get in Ernesto's face over the issue. But he had an absurd fear that the big man would grab Ernesto's shirtfront and lift him off his feet. Then he'd yell, "Hey *muchacho*, how come you're not a *Zapatista*?"

"Uh, hi, Mr. Ibarra," Ernesto said in a voice about an octave higher than normal. He glanced up at the sky, which was filling with puffy little clouds with dark edges. "The weatherman said it might rain. I guess that's good. We need the rain," Ernesto rattled on. Talking about the weather was always safe.

But Ernesto feared the topic would change from the weather swiftly. He dreaded having to explain himself to the big man. Ernesto knew Ibarra was best for the people of the *barrio*. But he was putting his personal romantic relationship ahead of his civic duty. Ernesto really didn't know how he would explain himself. Anything he had to say would sound lame at best and downright despicable at worst. In his mind, he tried to construct a script in case Mr. Ibarra asked.

"Yeah," the script went, "I know the whole *barrio* needs you man. But, see, I got this babe, Naomi Martinez, and she's related to that jerk Esposito. What's worse, Naomi's father is a bear, and he's tight with Esposito. So the deal is I gotta keep my chick and her family happy. You understand, right dude?'

"Hey Ernie," Mr. Ibarra said, interrupting the boy's unspoken speech. "You're looking good, *muchacho*. Lotta muscle. Carmen told me you're ripped. I see what she was saying. You're bustin' outta that T-shirt."

"Thanks," Ernesto replied, giddily happy to be talking about anything but the election. "I run a lot, and I'm exercising.

It's fun. I've put on some weight too, mostly muscle, I guess." That was all Ernesto could think of saying. He thought, "Now here comes the big question. It has to be coming now." Again, the script starting running silently in his mind.

"So why aren't you supporting me, Ernesto?" Mr. Ibarra was sure to ask. "Your parents were at the fund-raiser at Hortencia's, but I didn't see you. Oscar Perez made beautiful music. Everybody was there. How come you were missing, *muchacho*? How come you're not on board for this?"

But he didn't. Instead, he asked about the track team. "I gotta come see you at the next track meet," Mr. Ibarra promised. "Carmen told me you did great at the last one. Only one to beat you was that Avila boy. He runs like the wind. Oh, hey, Ernesto, I'm glad I run into you."

"Uh-oh!" Ernesto thought. He stopped breathing, and he thought his heart stopped too. "Here it finally comes."

But it didn't. "We're having a birthday party for Carmen at our house next Saturday," Mr. Ibarra said. "You gotta come. You remember when you came to that party before at our house? Well, you be sure to come for this and help us celebrate *mi hija*'s big day. Be sure to bring Naomi. Last time she couldn't come to our party because she was with Clay Aguirre. I don't let guys like that in my house. But you and Naomi come. Oscar Perez, he might just drop in too. He comes to the *barrio* every chance he gets 'cause he's sweet on your *Tía* Hortencia."

"Hey, thanks! I'd love to come," Ernesto answered when he started breathing again. "Naomi will be happy to come too. She and Carmen are real close."

"Yeah," Mr. Ibarra remarked, "my little girl, Carmen, she's gonna be seventeen. I can't believe it. To me she is *mi pequeña hija*, but she is seventeen!"

"She's a wonderful girl," Ernesto told him. "Everybody at school loves her."

"*Gracias, muchacho*," Mr. Ibarra responded, beaming and turning to go. "Oh, one more thing . . ." The man swung back to face Ernesto.

"Oh no!" Ernesto thought, stiffening. "I thought I was off the hook. But here it comes. The pitch. 'Why don't you join the campaign, Ernesto? You and Naomi should get on the team . . .'"

"There's going to be a surprise at the party," Mr. Ibarra asserted. "Nobody knows, not even Conchita, *mi esposa*. Your *amigo*, Abel Ruiz, is coming early to the party, and he's making some of the food. He is very excited. He told me he made a salmon dinner for your family and his, and it was wonderful. So I asked Abel, 'You make something for *mi hija*'s party too.' He usually doesn't do Mexican food. But this time he's making special Mexican treats. Conchita will be so jealous." The man laughed a big, booming laugh that echoed off the school building walls.

Carmen appeared then. "Hi Ernie, did Papa invite you to my party?" she asked.

"Yeah and I'm coming. Thanks," Ernesto responded. "I wouldn't miss it for the world."

"Remember," Carmen said. "Everybody will be there to have fun. No gifts! I don't want gifts. My gift will be having all my friends there to help me celebrate."

"No gifts from Papa either?" Mr. Ibarra asked, making a face.

"No Papa," Carmen chuckled. "That doesn't mean you." Carmen and Mr. Ibarra bid good-bye to Ernesto. Then they climbed into the Oldsmobile and drove away.

Ernesto couldn't believe Emilio Zapata Ibarra did not once mention the council race. The man had class!

Ernesto stood by his Volvo a few minutes waiting for Naomi. He was taking her home today. Naomi finally came, lugging several books. "Sorry I'm late, Ernie," she apologized. "But I had to get these books by Eudora Welty from the library."

"You know about Carmen's party, huh?" Ernesto asked.

"Yeah. She's turning seventeen. I won't turn seventeen until early next year," Naomi replied.

"It's gonna be March for me," Ernesto said. "Carmen said no gifts, but we gotta get her something. I'd feel funny going empty-handed to the party."

"Yeah," Naomi agreed. "I've been thinking the same thing ever since she told me. She's so nice. I really love her. There were times when things were really horrible at my house. Then Carmen would ask me to sleep over at her place. That helped loads. But all the time I was with Clay, Mr. Ibarra wouldn't let me and Clay come to parties. And I couldn't come without Clay. I couldn't blame Mr. Ibarra either. Clay can get really nasty, and he doesn't mind spoiling a party with his cracks."

"Yeah," Ernesto said. "The other night Clay came in the pizzeria. He started bad-mouthing poor little Yvette Ozono, calling her a gang girl and stuff. All of a sudden everybody's yelling. Poor Bashar comes racing out of the kitchen thinking war is breaking out. Clay has a way of makin' stuff like that happen."

"Yeah," Naomi agreed but wanted to change the subject. "Hey, Ernie, why don't we go to the mall now and get something for Carmen? I'm in no hurry to go home and hear another lecture about ungrateful children." Naomi did her girlish imitation of her father's gruff voice. "Kids who don't listen to their fathers are the scourge of mankind!"

They both laughed at her poor imitation. Then Naomi asked, "And you don't have to work at the pizzeria tonight do you?"

"No, I don't. Great idea, Naomi," Ernesto said, jumping at it. Not only did he not have a clue about what to get for Carmen, but any chance to spend time with Naomi was a gift for him. Off they went for the mall.

With the Volvo parked in the lot, they headed for the stores. The big store, which was the hub, was the first one they entered. But they hurried through it. "This place is too expensive," Naomi commented. The salesclerks outnumbered the customers. The good-looking salespeople, all dressed in signature black outfits, looked like mannequins. "You can get almost the same stuff they have in here for half the price in another store," Naomi said.

Ernesto looked at a graphic T-shirt. "Wow, fifty bucks for a T-shirt."

Naomi laughed. "That's what I mean!"

As they walked into a smaller store inside the mall, Ernesto asked, "Everything going okay at home, Naomi?"

"Yeah," Naomi responded, poking through a rack of girls' tops. "Dad doesn't drink much during the week. He knows he's got to be sharp to operate that equipment. In the beginning, he only worked a forklift. Now he does the heavy equipment. And you don't operate heavy equipment with a hangover. The weekends are what I dread. Dad's mad about something, he just drinks and drinks. And he gets meaner and meaner. I just pray for something good to happen. We need something to get his mind off grumping about his horrible children and poor Mom. According to him, she caused it all by letting us run wild."

Ernesto just nodded, again feeling sorry for Naomi. He couldn't imagine life in the Martinez house. His home was so different. His family was so different. Ernesto didn't know how he'd cope with what Naomi was dealing with.

When they reached the jewelry counter, Naomi said, "Oh, Carmen loves turquoise. She's been wanting a nice turquoise neck-lace to go with her scoop-necked tops. I bet she'd love this. It's kind of expensive. What do you say we go in on it together? Then we can both sign the card, and it won't break our budgets."

"Cool," Ernesto agreed. "I'm so glad you know what she likes. I was gonna end up getting her perfume or something. And I know I'd get the wrong kind, and she'd hate it." Then he asked, "Do you know what Carmen's parents are getting her?"

"It's a great big secret, Ernie," Naomi almost whispered, her violet eyes glowing with excitement. "You gotta promise me on your life that you won't tell if I share it."

"Promise," Ernesto said, in a low tone, as someone would overhear him.

"Well," Naomi began. She'd been bursting to tell someone. "Carmen got her driver's license, and she's been driving the family car." Naomi was almost squealing. "But you know, of course she wants a car. She's got that little job at the boutique, but she earns chump change there. Well, they're buying her a car, Ernie."

"Wow!" Ernesto exclaimed. "That'll blow her mind."

"It's a used car, of course," Naomi went on. "But Carmen's mom told me it's a cute little red convertible. They bought it from some guy that Carmen's dad knows. The car has been in the family for a while, and it's really in good shape. Their daughter moved away for college, and it's just sitting there gathering dust. The Ibarras got an incredibly good deal on it, 'cause Mr. Ibarra has done that family a lot of favors."

"Oh man!" Ernesto responded, feeling guilty again for not being a *Zapatista*. Mr. Ibarra was such a good guy.

"They're gonna hide the car in the garage," Naomi explained. "And they're gonna put some little tiny gift in a box, so Carmen thinks this is it. Then they'll ask Carmen to go in the garage and get something. And there'll be the convertible with a big bow on the top!"

With Carmen's present gift wrapped, they left the mall for the car. As they walked, Ernesto felt as though he needed to get something off his chest.

"Naomi," he began, as they approached the Volvo, "I hope Mr. Ibarra wins the election. I really do."

"Me too," Naomi affirmed. "Right now the polls show him ahead. But you can't tell what'll happen between now and election day. I keep fearing some smear campaign or something. Esposito's flyers are getting more personal. Mr. Ibarra's flyers just talk about the good stuff he's going to do. And Esposito is already putting out attack ads."

"Doesn't mudslinging end up hurting the person who's throwing the mud?" Ernesto asked.

"Sometimes," Naomi responded, "and sometimes, if you throw enough mud, some of it sticks. That's one of the big things I hate about politics. If everybody just stated their positions and stuff, it'd be okay. But they use these horrible pictures of their opponents. They take little sentences out of a paragraph. Then they get a whole different meaning from what the person really said."

"You know, Naomi," Ernesto commented, "I was reading this book the other day, *Profiles in Courage*. It was written by President John F. Kennedy when he was a young man. It talked about really courageous things that individual senators did, even though it cost them a lot in support, in their careers."

"I've heard of that book, but I never read it," Naomi remarked.

"Well, there was this one guy, Senator Grimes," Ernesto explained. "I think he was from Iowa. He really didn't like President Andrew Johnson, but he thought it would hurt the country if Johnson got impeached. Grimes, he'd just had a stroke, and he was really frail. But the vote on impeachment was coming up, and four guys carried him into the senate. Everybody told Grimes that, if he voted against impeachment, everybody would hate him. They'd say he was a traitor."

They were almost to the car, as Ernesto continued. "Grimes was pale and sick, but he voted against impeachment. And he saved the president from impeachment by that one vote. All his friends turned against him. They made effigies of him and burned them in public. He died with everybody hating him. But he said that he died at peace 'cause he followed his conscience. I read that stuff Naomi, and I feel creepy."

Naomi stopped walking and turned to face Ernesto. "You want to join those *Zapatistas*, don't you, Ernie? But you won't because of my father and the problems you think that would cause between us."

"Naomi, you mean more to me than—" Ernesto started to say. Naomi reached up with her fingers and put them over Ernesto's lips.

"Ernie," she told him, "I don't want to mean more to you than your conscience. What's going on in my house, I've got to deal with that. I don't want to put it on you, Ernie. You gotta be the best person you can be. Whatever happens, whatever comes, nothing is going to hurt *us*, Ernie. You've got to believe that."

When they reached the car, Ernesto took Naomi in his arms. They stood, hugging and kissing, for several minutes. Neither of them said a word.

Ernesto and Naomi arrived about fifteen minutes early for Carmen's birthday party at the little house on Nuthatch Lane. There was a sign out front with balloons tied to it. It read, "Carmen Ibarra is *diez y siete*!"

Ernesto and Naomi glanced at the closed garage and thought about the red convertible inside it. They both smiled.

The house was filled with Carmen's friends from school. Ernesto knew everybody. Julio Avila was there with Carlos and Dom, Jorge Aguilar, and Eddie Gonzales from the track team. Yvette Ozono was there with Tessie Zamora. Tessie had been in a wheelchair because of an accident but now hobbled around on crutches. Abel Ruiz had come with his girlfriend, Claudia Villa, but he had vanished into the kitchen. Carmen's cousin, Oscar Perez didn't bring his band. But he did bring his guitar and his beautiful voice to serenade the birthday girl.

Emilio Zapata Ibarra wore a red satin shirt, and his wife, Conchita, wore her beautiful red ruffled dress. They were ready for dancing. The atmosphere was warm and festive.

"I said no gifts!" Carmen complained as the pile of gifts on the kitchen table grew.

"We couldn't help ourselves," Naomi said, hugging Carmen.

"Here's the gift from Mom and Dad," Carmen remarked, looking at the small box. "I told them I needed a new wallet. So I bet that's what's in there. I bet they got me a nice one."

"I bet they did," Ernesto agreed. Naomi nudged him and gave him a look that said, "Don't you dare give anything away!"

Abel Ruiz was in the kitchen with Carmen's mother, putting the finishing touches on the food. Carmen and Naomi kept Claudia company. She went to a nearby private school, not Cesar Chavez High School. So she didn't know anybody there but Abel. Within minutes, Claudia was laughing and joking with the other girls as if she went to Chavez too.

"Abel is gonna be a big chef someday," Ernesto told Claudia. "He'll be on TV with his own program I bet."

"He loves to cook," Claudia said. "Whoever marries Abel is gonna be so lucky. No being stuck in the kitchen for his wife!"

Abel, wearing a big puffy chef's hat, emerged from the kitchen with a tray of appetizers. Conchita followed him with two more trays he had assembled. The trays were crammed with appetizers. They were little seafood canapés, filled with shrimp, crab, and lobster with *cotija* cheese and a heavenly mango salsa.

"Ta-dah!" Abel cried, enjoying every minute.

The party was underway!

Toward the end of the party, after Oscar Perez sang a sweet song to Carmen, she opened her gifts. She raved over all of them, especially the turquoise necklace from Naomi and Ernesto. She praised even the smallest token gifts. Oscar Perez gave her a lovely gold necklace. But when Carmen opened the package from her parents, there was just a little ladybug pin.

"Oh, it's so cute," Carmen exclaimed. But Ernesto could tell she was surprised, maybe even a little disappointed.

"Carmen, *mi hija*," Mr. Ibarra told her. "There is one more little thing for you in the garage. We forgot to bring it in the house."

"Yes," Conchita added, "in all the excitement we forgot to wrap it. It's still out there in the garage."

Carmen looked puzzled. She looked from her father to her mother.

"Come outside, *mi hija*," Mr. Ibarra suggested. "It is dark in the garage, and we shall open it up."

The Ibarras and all the guests followed Carmen as she went outside and pressed the garage door opener. Slowly the door rose. Carmen began to scream. People across the street came rushing out to see why a girl was screaming.

Carmen leaped into her father's arms, and he lifted her up as if she were four years old instead of seventeen. He kissed her. And her mother kissed her. Passing cars slowed in the street to see what all the excitement was about.

Carmen Ibarra was sitting in her red convertible, still screaming and laughing and crying when most of the guests went home.

CHAPTER SEVEN

When Ernesto got home from school the following Thursday, he sensed something strange the moment he entered the house. Ernesto didn't see his mother, *Abuela,* Katalina, or Juanita. Nobody was in the front room, but he felt a charged atmosphere, as if something significant had happened. He heard a low-key commotion somewhere in the house, and he followed the noise to the den. A sliding glass door in the den opened into the patio. They were all out there.

Mom had heard the door slam, and she called out, "Ernie?"

"Yeah Mom," Ernesto responded, stressed by the strangeness of the house.

The first person Ernesto saw was Mom. "They came!" she cried, holding out a colorful object. "Look!"

"The book!" Ernesto snatched it from his mother. He stared at the bright cover. On it was the pit bull named Thunder, who was a dead ringer for Brutus. The cat that looked just like the Sandoval cat, Calico, was also there. In the book, though, the cat was named Princess. The title of the book was *Thunder and Princess*.

"Oh Mom!" Ernesto cried. "It looks terrific." He started flipping through the pages, admiring the funny, whimsical pictures. "That guy, the illustrator, he did a fabulous job. Wow, congratulations, Mom!"

Katalina was hugging one of the books to her chest. "I'm taking it to school tomorrow, Mom," she swore. "I'm showing it to everybody."

Juanita had one of the books too. She was dancing around the room, clutching it. "You gotta come to my room and read from the book, Mama," she insisted.

"We're all so proud of you, Maria," *Abuela* told her, a book on her lap. "When I go to mass on Sunday and we go over to the hall for coffee, I'm showing it to all the ladies. They will be so impressed."

"Has Dad seen it yet?" Ernesto asked, just now realizing that his father wasn't home yet.

"No," Mom replied. "When he comes home, he'll see it for the first time. I called my parents and told them the books came. I promised to send them copies, but they can't wait. They're coming down tonight. They'll have dinner with us. They were so thrilled."

Ernesto looked at the author's name on the book: Maria Sandoval. He was so happy for his mother. She was a wonderful wife to Dad and a great mother to Ernesto and the girls. And he was proud of her for all that. But he could now be proud because she was making a dream come true. Mom had graduated from high school with high honors. She had been voted the student most likely to accomplish important things. Her parents imagined their only daughter—their only child—as a college professor or a CEO of a large company. She was smart, charming, and beautiful. There were no limits to where she could go, they thought.

Mom's parents, Eva and Alfredo Vasquez (especially Eva) always felt a tinge of regret that she had not accomplished greater things. Yes, their daughter had a very happy marriage. Yes, she had chosen a fine man to be her husband. Yes, she had beautiful, healthy children, and another on the way. Yet they were a little sad because she might have accomplished so much more had her star been allowed to rise as far as it could go.

Ernesto hugged and kissed his mother. "Mom, I'm so proud of you. I've always been proud of you, but this is amazing. They say half the people in the country would like to get a book published. And you did it!"

Ernesto's mother was flushed with happiness. "Thanks sweetheart," she said.

"I'm proud of you too, Mama," Katalina piped up.

"I'm so proud I could burst," Juanita declared shrilly, jumping up and down to stress the point.

Luis Sandoval pulled into the driveway about twenty minutes later. Ernesto's mother ran to the car before he even opened the garage door. "Luis!" she cried "My book! The copies came today. My mom and dad are driving down for dinner tonight. They're so excited they can't wait to see the book."

Luis Sandoval turned off the engine and forgot all about opening the garage door for the moment. He jumped out of the car and grabbed his wife. He lifted her off her feet and spun around with her in his arms. Then he looked at the book. "How beautiful—ah—Maria Sandoval. *Querida mia*," he said softly, as if it were a song, a love song.

Ernesto then remembered something. He remembered who had inspired the idea for the book: the pit bull at the Martinez house—Brutus. "Mom," he said, "Grandpa and Grandma won't be here for more than an hour. Could I take one of the books over to Naomi and her family right now?"

"Sure, sweetheart," Mom replied. "I have twenty-five author's copies. Give them one."

"But you gotta sign it, Mom. You know, autograph it," Ernesto insisted.

Mom laughed. "Oh dear. Being a celebrity is very intimidating. What shall I say?"

"Uh, let's see," Ernesto thought out loud. "'To Naomi Martinez and her family, and to Brutus.' Yeah, that's it Mom."

Ernesto grabbed the book as soon as his mother autographed it. Naomi lived on Bluebird Street, which was right next to Wren where Ernie lived. So he jogged over, the book under his arm. He ran down Tremayne Street and turned onto Bluebird.

He could see the Martinez house. Felix Martinez's pickup truck was in the driveway. Good! Ernesto hoped that seeing the book based on his beloved pit bull would improve his grumpy mood. Ernesto was breathless when he turned into the Martinez yard and ran to the door, hitting the bell.

"Ernie!" Linda Martinez exclaimed when she came to the door. "What on earth? Is something wrong? You look like you've been running."

"Mrs. Martinez, can I come in?" Ernesto asked.

"Sure, Ernie," she said.

Felix Martinez yelled from the living room, where he was watching television. "Who is it? If that idiot pest control salesman came back, tell him to get lost."

"It's Ernie, Felix," Mrs. Martinez responded.

"Where's Naomi?" Ernesto asked.

"She's in her room, working on a PowerPoint for her English report on that

Eudora Welty," Mrs. Martinez answered. Then she turned and hollered down the hallway to the bedrooms. "Oh Naomi! Ernie is here."

Naomi came out and took one look at Ernesto's glowing face. "Ernie—what?" she asked.

Ernesto held up the book. "Mom's book came out!"

"Ohhh!" Naomi cried, grabbing the book. "Look at the cover! It's Brutus and your cat, Calico! Look, Mom! Dad! Here's the book Maria Sandoval based on our dog!"

Felix Martinez came in from the living room. He took the book from Naomi. "Hey, it's a real book," he noted, as if he expected something homemade, maybe in a spiral binder. Mr. Martinez turned the first page. "Hey, she autographed it. Look what she wrote, 'To Naomi Martinez and her family and to Brutus.'" Felix Martinez laughed. He didn't laugh much, and Naomi was glad to see him laugh. "Hey, ain't that somethin'? Hey Brutus, look here. You're famous.

Linda Martinez looked at the book then. "This is marvelous," she remarked. "Oh Ernie, your mom must be thrilled."

"Yeah, she is," Ernesto said. "When Mom was a young girl, she planned to be a writer. She even got some stuff published in magazines. Then she got busy with us kids. But she's always had her dream in the back of her mind."

Linda Martinez looked thoughtful. "I wanted to be a nurse when I was a young girl. That's what I wanted, but there wasn't enough money for college. I guess I've nursed my own kids enough times to say I'm sort of a nurse."

"You bet, Mom," Naomi assured her. "When I got pneumonia, you saved my life. Remember that winter I was so sick with pneumonia?"

Linda Martinez nodded. She ran her finger over the name "Maria Sandoval." "You tell your mother she can really be proud of this, Ernie."

"I gotta go home now," Ernesto said. "My grandparents are driving down from Los Angeles to see the book."

When Ernesto went outside for the short jog home, Naomi followed him. "Thanks for the book, Ernie. Thanks for bringing it over right away. That meant a lot to Dad. It's like you respected him. You made Dad laugh too. That was nice." Naomi stood on tiptoe and kissed Ernesto. "See you in school tomorrow, babe."

Ernesto jogged back to Wren Street, a happy smile on his face.

The Vasquezes, in their Dodge Caravan, pulled into the Sandoval driveway at seven forty-five. Eva Vasquez came in first, with her husband, Alfredo, bringing up the rear. She quickly embraced her daughter and then demanded, "Where is it? Where's the book?"

"Here Gramma," Katalina said, thrusting the book at her grandmother. As she looked at the author's name, for just a second Eva showed disappointment on her face. She had been hoping the name would be Maria Vasquez Sandoval. But then she shrugged and brightened, holding the book at arm's length and admiring it. "Oh, it's lovely. The cover art is magical."

Alfredo Vasquez hugged his daughter. "Maria, congratulations! This is such an accomplishment. In today's publishing market for a first-time author to get a book like this out. It's impressive."

The Vasquezes both paged through the book with great interest. Then, finally, everyone sat down to dinner.

"Oh Maria, can we take several copies home?" her mother asked.

"Of course, Mom. I've got a lot of them," Mom responded.

Eva Vasquez began to smirk. "I want to show the books to all our friends. Maria, do you remember Liddy Paterno?"

"Sure, Mom," Maria Sandoval said.

"Liddy's parents moved to Los Angeles like we did," Eva explained to the others at the table. "Liddy's mom, Ceci, she lives close to us. She goes on and on about all her daughter's accomplishments. Liddy went to college, of course, and got good grades."

"She was always smart," Ernesto's mother added.

"Not as smart as you were, darling," Eva Vasquez objected. "You graduated from high school number two in the class, and Liddy was number six. Anyway, Liddy got this job with a fashion magazine in New York, and Ceci was ecstatic. She kept showing me Liddy's name in the front of the magazine. Well, la-di-da! Liddy was going to be a big editor and who knows what else? Both you girls had writing aspirations, of course. Here's Liddy on the staff of this major fashion mag. And here you are back in the *barrio* raising your kids, not doing much of anything."

Ernesto was having trouble enjoying his *carne asada*. Grandma Eva had obviously been suffering all these years. Her beautiful, talented daughter was wasting her gifts on being a mother and wife. This Liddy person was apparently setting the New York fashion world on fire. She was giving her mother bragging rights that rankled Mom's mother.

"Well," Eva Vasquez continued, "when the economic downturn came along, didn't little Liddy lose her job. Now she's scratching out a living doing temp work. And here you are, Maria, a professional writer with a beautiful book published. Well, just wait until I show this book to Ceci. All these years she's been rubbing it in that her daughter achieved the success she was destined for. In the meantime, my daughter was languishing in the *barrio*."

To Ernesto, Grandma Eva sounded as though she was rejoicing in the professional disaster that overtook her friend's daughter. Ernesto always suspected that *Abuela* Eva was a bit of a social climber. She was one of those mothers Ernesto saw in the supermarket. They were the ones bragging that their three-year-old was accepted in the best preschool in town, Maybe another kid was being watched by a second-rate mom-and-pop operation. But Ernesto had never seen his grandmother display this side of her so flagrantly.

Ernesto saw that his mother looked embarrassed, her head lowered as she ate her *carne asada*. Ernesto didn't even want to look at his father. When he did, he saw that Luis Sandoval had a strange, almost robotic look on his face. Eva's speech seemed to have driven him into a Zen-like mood. He had tuned everything out.

Finally Ernesto's father looked up with a faint smile. "It's interesting," he said very quietly, "how the idea for the book came from our neighbors on the next street, the Martinez family. They got this pit bull, and the wife was terrified of it. She even locked herself in the kitchen when the dog was loose. Turned out, though, that the dog was friendly. Now Mrs. Martinez loves him."

Eva Vasquez's eyes became glazed over at the discussion of the genesis for the book. She was waiting for her chance to gather information. Looking at her daughter, she inquired, "Of course there will be more books. I imagine your agent is already after you to do another one. Perhaps a larger one, like those Harry Potter books that were all the rage a few years ago. I'm sure you could do even better with that sort of a book."

Luis Sandoval continued to speak softly. "The neighbor's dog is named Brutus. But Maria changed that to Thunder in the book."

Eva Vasquez looked at her son-in-law and asked, "What did you say, Luis?"

"Uh, nothing," Ernesto's father replied. "Do you want more salsa, Mother?"

"No, thank you," Eva declined. "So, Maria, what is your agent saying about future plans?"

"Mom, the book just came out," Mom explained. "So we'll have to wait and see."

"But there *will* be other books," Eva persisted. "This is only the beginning, darling. Oh, you know, we have a little group of friends. We have lunch every Thursday, and

Ceci comes. I can't wait to see her face when I show her this book. She is just going to turn as green as grass!" She turned to her husband, "Al, did you ever see such a striking cover? I'm sure parents will just snap the book up for their children."

"Absolutely!" Alfredo Vasquez affirmed.

Ernesto smiled to himself. His grandmother was clearly the boss in that family. Grandfather Alfredo seemed almost as intimidated by his spouse as Linda Martinez was by Felix.

Alfredo Vasquez turned to Ernesto's father then and asked, "So how are things going at Chavez High, Luis?"

"Very well," Dad responded, relieved to be on another subject. "I'm enjoying my classes. I've been trying to lure some of the dropouts back into school. I'm having a fair amount of success. This one girl, she was out of school for some time and—"

"I would imagine you'll be making some appearances at bookstores," Eva

Vasquez interrupted, drowning out her son-in-law's voice. "Perhaps you'll even be interviewed on television. Local stations at first, but then who knows where it all may lead."

"This girl," Luis Sandoval persisted, "had a tragic experience, losing a loved one to gang violence. But now she's back in school and doing very well. She's acing some difficult math classes."

"And perhaps you'll be speaking at some of these large educational conferences," Eva Vasquez continued, her eyes glowing. "I wouldn't be surprised if you were speaking all over the country, talking to the teachers. A book like this, it's bound to spur enthusiasm for reading in young children. They *do* like dogs and cats, and those characters are so cute."

She turned then and looked at her son-in-law. "Were you saying something, Luis?"

"No, no," Ernesto's father responded. "I was just wondering if you wanted more salsa."

"Actually, I hate salsa," Eva Vasquez declared. "Al and I have gotten away from all that Mexican food we used to eat as children. We prefer Thai food now."

"I'll take more salsa," Alfredo Vasquez requested.

"Mommy is coming to my classroom to talk to my second grade," Juanita piped up, struggling to get into the conversation.

"That's nice, sweetie," Grandma Vasquez replied. "But your mama has much bigger fish to fry I expect." She winked at Maria.

"You gonna fry some fish, Mama?" Juanita asked.

Ernesto started to laugh. Then he quickly recovered his composure and took some more salsa for himself. His eyes met Alfredo's eyes, and they had a moment of understanding.

"I must text some of the other girls you used to go to school with," Eva Vasquez said. "None of them ever had a book published. They won't believe it. Oh Maria, I just knew you would shine when the right opportunity came along. I knew you would live up to the great dreams your father and I had for you. We always knew you would be our little star. Didn't we think that, Alfred?"

"Indeed," the man responded in a bland voice.

Maria Sandoval looked over at her husband. He smiled. Mom started to giggle a little. Then she couldn't stop.

"*What?*" Eva Vasquez asked.

"You sure you don't want more salsa, Mama?" Luis Sandoval responded.

CHAPTER EIGHT

When Ernesto Sandoval walked onto the campus of Chavez High School on the following Thursday, he saw something he had never seen before. A group of students were surrounding Carmen Ibarra, and she was crying. Carmen was a tough girl, and Ernesto had never seen her even near tears. But now her shoulders were heaving with sobs. Ernesto ran over to where the small crowd gathered. "Carmen," he gasped, "what's the matter?"

Yvette Ozono was one of the students comforting Carmen. She handed Ernesto a crude-looking flyer, which was headed, "The Truth About Emilio Ibarra." Ernesto read the brief message.

> Ibarra was a gangbanger as a youth. He
> was mixed up in gang warfare and drug
> dealing. He used crack cocaine, and he was
> involved in a drive-by shooting. . . .

The poorly produced flyer went on, but the message was clear. The candidate for city council had a dark past, which he had managed to conceal until now.

"What?" Ernesto cried. "Who did this?"

Carmen wiped her eyes with the back of her hand and started explaining. "Oh Ernie, they're all over the school and in some stores. They're even nailed to fences and palm trees. Some people must have been out all night putting them out. It's all a horrible lie, a smear, but some people are going to believe it! It's so wrong! It's so evil!"

Julio Avila was also in the crowd of kids. His eyes were narrow and angry. "Esposito will stop at nothing so he can keep his job. He's done nothing for the people, yet he wants to stay there. My father's friend, Rezzi, he told my father the man is totally corrupt, and this proves it!"

"You think Monte Esposito did this?" Ernesto asked.

"His friends did," Abel Ruiz replied bitterly. "His supporters. Esposito is sneaky enough to steer clear of it. He's a wily little rat. He'll probably even make some phony statement denouncing the flyer. But you better believe he knew about it and approved it."

Ernesto bunched up the flyer that was in his hand. A rage engulfed him that he never felt before. "*Basta!*" he cried. "*Basta!* No more. Enough. I won't stand on the sidelines anymore! Abel, you got those Ibarra flyers in your car? I want a bunch of them when I leave school today."

"I got a bunch too," Yvette said.

"After school," Ernesto vowed, his heart pounding, "I'm passing them out everywhere. I'm talking to people every chance I get. I'll go up and down Washington and Tremayne. I'll hit all the residential streets, Cardinal and Bluebird, all of them. This is too much!"

Carmen drew close to Ernesto and gave him a hug.

"My dad has known Emilio Ibarra for most of his life," Ernesto cried. "They've been friends since they were kids. He was never in any gangs. That's crazy! Mr. Ibarra is an honorable man. He hates drugs. He's done so much as a private citizen to steer kids away from gangs and drugs. What a stinking smear!"

"They're desperate," Dom Reynosa remarked. "The polls look bad for them, and now they'll stoop to anything."

"Yeah," Carlos Negrete agreed. "Over on my street, little kids were passing these smear flyers out. Somebody gave them five dollars to plaster them all over the *barrio*. The kids were putting them on the windshields of parked cars."

Ernesto noticed Clay Aguirre standing nearby. He didn't come near the group of kids around Carmen, but he was watching and listening. Maybe, Ernesto thought darkly, Clay had done this. He was doing everything possible to get back in the good graces of Naomi. Maybe he thought, by running a smear campaign against Mr. Ibarra, he would gain the gratitude of Felix Martinez. Maybe he thought Mr. Martinez would then press Naomi to give Clay another chance. Even now, the father was telling his daughter that maybe she made a mistake in choosing Ernesto over Clay.

Ernesto was just angry enough to approach Clay with one of the smear flyers. "You seen these?" he demanded.

"Yeah," Clay answered. "Looks like somebody did a little digging, and some skeletons came tumbling out of old Ibarra's closet." Clay grinned. "Looks like squeaky-clean Emilio Ibarra isn't so clean after all."

"It's a smear," Ernesto countered. "It's all lies. Everybody in the *barrio* knows Ibarra. Most of his friends have known him since they were all kids together. He was never in any gang. He hates gangs. He's done more than anybody to clean up the gang problem."

Clay smirked and put on a mockingly thoughtful face. "Remember when we were doin' Shakespeare in old Hunt's class? What was the line? Oh yeah. 'He doth protest too much.' Maybe that's why Ibarra's so hung up on gangs. He knows them from the inside out. He used to run with them, seems like."

"Did you make these flyers, Aguirre?" Ernesto demanded. "This looks like something low enough for you to do."

Clay laughed. Ernesto had a terrible urge to punch him in the face, but he wasn't fool enough to do that. As Ernesto turned, he saw Naomi arriving. She had seen Ernesto and Clay yelling at each other, and she looked shocked.

"What's going on?" Naomi asked, looking at Ernesto.

Clay answered her before Ernesto could. "Seems like a great big ugly skeleton just jumped out of Ibarra's closet, Naomi. He used to be 18th Street. He kinda led a double life. Being a good kid by day and going to school, gangbanger by night, getting

145

into wars, dealing drugs. It's all here." Clay handed Naomi a flyer.

"It's a smear campaign. None of this is true," Ernesto said. "Some creeps connected to Esposito's campaign put these out to stop Ibarra from running away with the election like the polls say he's doing."

Naomi glanced at the flyer. "Most people in the *barrio* have known Emilio Ibarra all their lives," she commented. "The older people knew him as a child. This is ridiculous."

"No, it's true," Clay insisted. "A couple former gangbangers who used to hang out with Ibarra told the whole story. Yeah, Ibarra put up a good front when he was a teenager. But when nighttime came, the skunk roamed, shooting up the *barrio,* dealing crack cocaine."

"Clay Aguirre," Carmen screamed, "You're a dirty liar. How dare you lie like that about my father? How many people around here can tell you good stories about my dad? He reached out to them and helped them when they needed a hand. You're a snake, Clay Aguirre. I hate you!"

Ms. Hunt was on her way to English class when she noticed the commotion. "What's this?" she asked. "You people should be going to classes, not standing here screaming at each other!"

"Ms. Hunt, look," Carmen responded, thrusting one of the smear flyers at the teacher. "These are all over the school. They're in the streets and on peoples' cars in the parking lot. Somebody just papered the *barrio* with these filthy lies about my father! He's ahead in the election, and they did this to try to stop him."

Ms. Hunt scanned at the crude flyer and spoke to the group of kids. "This is a disgrace. In the first place, it's strictly against school rules to pass out political literature on campus. We don't let kids even wear political T-shirts. We certainly don't want scurrilous flyers like this one. I intend to investigate who's passing these out. If a student is behind this, that person will be suspended."

Ms. Hunt liked Ernesto. He was a good student and a responsible young man. She often relied on him. "Ernesto, grab a dozen of your friends right now and cover the campus. Pick up every one of these. Bring them to my classroom so that they can be disposed of. I'm showing them to Ms. Sanchez so that the principal knows what a gross violation of school rules has taken place."

Ernesto turned to the kids standing around and gave the order. "Let's go, you guys."

"Too late!" Clay laughed. "Most of the flyers are already in automobiles and binders. People are gonna read 'em. That sucking noise you hear is support for Emilio Ibarra going down the drain."

Ernesto ignored Clay. He knew that if he listened to Clay another few seconds, he'd have to deck him. Ernesto wasn't about to get thrown out of Chavez High for getting into a fight with a creep like Aguirre.

Ernesto and his crew found about a hundred flyers and brought them to Ms. Hunt's room. They even dug them out of trash cans. That way, no curious students could fish them out and read them.

After school, Naomi came up to Ernesto's Volvo in the parking lot. "Did you mean what you said, Ernie?" she asked.

Ernesto's head was spinning. He had said a lot of things. He was so angry he felt as though he had a fever. "Did I mean what?" he asked.

"You said you were joining the Ibarra campaign. Carmen told me you said you wouldn't stand on the sidelines anymore. Did you mean that?" Naomi asked.

"Yeah, Naomi, I meant it," Ernesto said. "I got a bunch of Ibarra flyers in my car. Right after I take you home, I'm passing them out in stores, on the street, wherever I can. I won't stand for what's happened. It's just too much. *Basta!*"

"You don't have to drop me off," Naomi told him.

"No, I don't like you walking home alone," Ernesto insisted.

"I didn't mean I was walking home, Ernie," Naomi explained. "I want to help you pass out the flyers."

Ernesto looked at her. "Naomi, you don't have to do this. I don't want to get you in trouble with—"

"Abel told me you yelled *basta* when you saw those flyers," Naomi said. "Well, I feel the same way. Besides, I have to see Ms. Hunt a little later about my report."

Ernesto grabbed Naomi and hugged her. Then they got into the Volvo and headed out.

A lot of the smear flyers were lying in the street, in the gutters. Some were still stuck to telephone poles and tree trunks. Ernesto and Naomi picked them, ripped them down, and stashed them in the Volvo. The owner of a yogurt shop came out of his store holding one of the smear flyers. "You kids know anything about this stuff?" he asked them.

"Yeah," Ernesto answered. "It's part of a smear campaign that Councilman Esposito's supporters are running against Ibarra. Ibarra is a great guy, and everything in this flyer is a dirty lie."

"You mean this dude Ibarra wasn't no gang member?" the shop owner asked. "'Cause I was for him till I read this."

"It's not true. It's all lies," Ernesto asserted. "Emilio Ibarra is a great guy, and he'll be wonderful for the *barrio*."

The owner of the yogurt shop was young, about thirty, and a newcomer to the neighborhood. That's why he didn't know Emilio Ibarra's reputation.

"Here," Naomi said, handing the man one of Ibarra's campaign flyers. "Read this. It'll tell you all about Mr. Ibarra's background and all the people who're supporting him. It'll tell you what he wants to do for our community."

Ernesto and Naomi covered Tremayne Street between Cardinal and Bluebird. Carmen and Yvette canvassed Cardinal Street. Dom and Carlos took Wren, Finch, and Nuthatch. Julio Avila, Jorge Aguilar, and Eddie Gonzales covered Sparrow and Starling streets. They all met on Washington, having disposed of all the smear flyers they could find.

As the nine students came toward Cesar Chavez High School, Felix Martinez drove up in his pickup truck. Zack was sitting beside his father in the front seat. The truck pulled over to the curb, and Mr. Martinez's gaze swept the teenagers, focusing mainly on his daughter. His voice was cold as he spoke. "Somebody called me. Said did I know my girl was going with a gang of teenagers up and down the street rippin' up Monte Esposito's signs? He got permission to put up those signs. You kids got no right to be messing with 'em."

"We didn't touch any of Monte Esposito's campaign posters, Mr. Martinez," Ernesto responded politely. "We wouldn't do that. You're right. He has every right to get permission to put up signs in residential neighborhoods and in stores. Disturbing those signs would be vandalism, and we don't do that kinda thing. We've just been picking up this trash."

Ernesto handed Mr. Martinez one of the smear flyers. "These appeared all over school and the *barrio*. Mr. Martinez, you've known Emilio Ibarra all his life, and you know this isn't true."

Felix Martinez scanned the flyer. He looked up then and shrugged. "I didn't know the guy that well. He was younger than me and my crowd. He coulda done these things. I don't know. I can't swear to it that he didn't. Maybe somebody found out he had stuff to hide. Maybe somebody thought the people ought to know before they get an ex-gangbanger druggie in there. The voters got a right to know stuff like this."

"Dad," Naomi objected, "we've talked about the Ibarra family lots of times. You told me you'd see Emilio at football games. You'd talk about him even helping Padre Benito collect food for the Thanksgiving and Christmas drives. If something like this was going on, you would've known about it. A lot of people would have known."

Mr. Martinez was unfazed by Naomi's words. "I don't know what he mighta done when nobody was looking," he replied. "Y'hear what I'm sayin'. Yeah, he talked a good game, but maybe he was one of the 18th Street homies."

Felix Martinez then glared at his daughter. "But, hey, Naomi, what're you doing with this bunch of jokers? Monte Esposito is family. Don't that mean nothin' to you? You know how many times Monte's been sittin' at our table? You know what he's done for me. He got those playoff tickets, even got me in to see the president that time. Waddya doing with these *Zapatistas,* girl? You want to stab family in the back. That what you want to do here? Ain't it bad enough Orlando and Manny doin' that? Now you wanna turn the knife in my back?" His tone was bitter.

"Dad," Naomi persisted, "I wasn't going to get involved, but this smear campaign is just so evil. It's a terrible thing to put out lies like this. There comes a time when you just have to stand up for what's right."

Felix Martinez turned to his son. "Zack, you get in the pickup bed. Only room for two people in the cab, and your sister, she's riding home with me right now." Zack jumped out of the cab and obediently climbed into the bed of the pickup. Mr. Martinez opened the passenger side door and commanded his daughter. "Get in, Naomi. I ain't askin' you twice."

"I'll be home a little later, Dad," Naomi responded in a calm voice. Ernesto knew she had to be shaking inside. He felt so sorry for her. Here she was, standing in front of all her friends—Ernesto, her boyfriend, Carmen and Yvette, Julio and the other guys. Her father was treating her like a disobedient five-year-old. "I'm not ready to go home. I won't be late, Dad."

The others looked on uncomfortably, with pity for Naomi in their eyes. They all realized what a hard thing this was for her. She had never defied her father in any important way. Ernesto wanted to say or do something to help Naomi. But he didn't know what to say or do that wouldn't just make matters worse. If he criticized Mr. Martinez for humiliating his daughter, the man might just fly into a dangerous rage.

Finally, in a shaky voice, Ernesto offered, "Mr. Martinez, I'll bring Naomi home in a little while, okay?"

"You done enough already, *punk*," Felix Martinez spat out the words. He looked at Ernesto with something close to hatred. The glare made the boy's blood run cold.

But Mr. Martinez wasn't finished. "You wormed your way into my daughter's heart and into my family, Sandoval. What you ended up doing was turning my little girl against me, against her family. Don't you be telling me you're gonna bring Naomi home in your own sweet time. You got no business being with her at all. You're not man enough to have a girlfriend. You're a wimp and a coward, Sandoval. She's my kid, and I'm taking her home *now*. I'm doin' it if I gotta pick her up and toss her into the cab of the truck myself like she was a sack of potatoes."

The tension was so thick that it seemed to crackle like distant lightning just before a terrible storm.

"I'm sorry, Dad," Naomi said in soothing tone. "I can't go home with you right now. I have an appointment to go see Ms. Hunt, my English teacher. I promised her I'd let her see what I'm doing on my Eudora Welty paper. She's expecting me, Dad. She's staying after school for kids who want help with their reports. I'll be home in about an hour."

At a nodded command from his father, Zack scrambled back into the cab of the pickup. Felix Martinez gave his daughter a withering look and put the truck in gear. When he drove away, he left a long rubber track in the street from his spinning tires.

CHAPTER NINE

Ernesto and Naomi didn't say much to each other as they walked to Ms. Hunt's classroom. Naomi put her outline on the teacher's desk. Before Ms. Hunt looked it over, she commented on the mudslinging campaign. "The news media," she told the two students, "has gotten on the story of those nasty flyers. All the local TV stations will be reporting on them in the six o'clock news. It's quite a firestorm. Whoever dreamed this up didn't do Councilman Esposito any favors." She then offered Naomi some feedback on her outline.

When they were back in Ernesto's Volvo, Ernesto said, "Naomi, I'm worried

sick about you. What're you going to do?
I've never seen your father so angry."

"I'm going home, Ernie," Naomi asserted. "It's quarter to six, and I said I'd be
home within the hour."

"Naomi, I'm worried," Ernesto persisted.

Naomi reached over and put her hand
on Ernesto's arm. "Don't be worried about
me, babe. I'm fine. I really am."

Ernesto started the car and drove
slowly toward Bluebird Street. "I wish I
didn't have to drop you off there, Naomi.
Maybe I should go in the house with
you to make sure everything is okay," he
suggested.

Ernesto didn't want to spell it all out.
He didn't want to give voice to what was on
his mind. Felix Martinez was in a dark rage.
His daughter had defied him in front of all
her friends. Everybody would know now
that her father had lost control of his own
family. He was a man who was capable of
violence. He had struck his wife in the past.

159

Ernesto didn't want to let the girl he loved go into that house alone and face who knew what.

"Don't worry, Ernie," Naomi insisted as they turned on Bluebird Street and the house came into view. "He's my father. I've lived with him for sixteen years. It'll be fine."

Ernesto pulled into the driveway. "I could just sorta go in with you and maybe apologize or something," he said.

Naomi leaned over and put a quick kiss on Ernesto's lips.

"Call me later, okay? Please?" Ernesto begged.

"I will," Naomi assured him. She got out of the car when Ernesto opened the door for her.

"I could wait here just in case," Ernesto offered.

"See you at school tomorrow, Ernie," Naomi said. She walked briskly to the door and went inside. Brutus barked a greeting. Ernesto didn't want to pull out of the driveway, but he did. He had to. It was what she wanted. To do otherwise would have been to say he didn't trust her judgment.

Ernesto drove the short distance home, sick with worry. His imagination was working overtime. He thought Felix Martinez might lose it and hurt her. The thought of that was like a scalding pain in Ernesto's heart. He wanted desperately to back out of the driveway and speed over to Bluebird Street. He wanted to bang on the door and demand to see Naomi. He needed to know that she was safe. But he didn't do any such thing.

Ernesto was going into his house when his cell phone rang. "Ernie?" Naomi said.

"Babe, you okay?" Ernesto asked breathlessly.

"Yeah," she affirmed. "He called me Benedict Arnold. Remember Benedict Arnold who betrayed the colonies in the American Revolution? He glared at me and said I was a traitor too."

"And?" Ernesto asked.

"Then he got another beer," Naomi answered. "He's waiting for the evening news. He told Mom it's going to be all over the news that Emilio Ibarra has been exposed as a liar and a criminal. It's going to be the end of Ibarra's campaign. Uncle Monte's going to cruise to victory because there'll be so much contempt for Ibarra. Dad's really excited about seeing that on TV."

Ernesto breathed a long sigh of relief. "I love you, Naomi," he whispered into the phone.

"Love you too, Ernie," she responded.

Naomi sounded all right. Ernesto's conflicting emotions were overwhelming him. He had thought of Naomi as a sweet, lovely, but weak girl. He'd had no idea she could show so much courage. He had to get used to this different image of someone he loved. He was shocked at her courage and stunned with pride.

After dinner, the Sandoval family gathered in the living room to watch the evening news. The news anchor was a pretty young blonde, Gloria Hadley. Most local news anchorwomen were long on beauty and charm but short on real reportorial experience, Hadley, however, had been a real reporter; so her work had depth. She was competent, and she could be hard-hitting.

"The city council race," she began, "in which newcomer Emilio Ibarra is running to unseat veteran Councilman Monte Esposito, was thrown into turmoil today by the appearance of hundreds of campaign flyers making dramatic charges against Ibarra. The flyers were all over Cesar Chavez High School. Handing them out violated the school's policy against distributing political campaign material on campus. They were also on the streets and in stores."

Ms. Sanchez, the principal at Chavez High then appeared in a sound bite. She indignantly denounced the flyers. "To have our school used to spread anonymous and apparently unfounded charges angers and saddens all of us," she stated. Hadley was then back on screen and resumed her report.

"The accusations against Ibarra included the charges that he was a gang member as a youth and involved in criminal activities. No evidence was offered for these anonymous assertions. Reporters who talked with friends of Emilio Ibarra say that the charges "unbelievable" and "laughable." The firestorm over what seem to be false charges comes as part of a mudslinging effort late in the campaign. We spoke earlier with Councilman Esposito about this matter."

A split screen appeared, showing a video shot earlier in the day. Hadley was at a desk at the left, and Councilman Esposito was at the right.

"Councilman," Ms. Hadley began, "what is your response to this flyer that accuses your opponent of serious crimes as a youth?"

Councilman Esposito looked as though he had gained about twenty pounds since Ernesto last saw him on TV. He looked puffy and tired. "My people are not responsible for this," the councilman asserted. "We're running a clean campaign on the issues. We do not condone this sort of thing at all. I don't want to be associated with this stuff in any way. I am running for reelection because, with my experience, I can better serve the people than Mr. Ibarra,"

"Councilman," Ms. Hadley asked, "have you any idea where this flyer came from or who might have produced it?"

"No, no, no idea." Mr. Esposito waved his hands in front of him, palms up. He seemed to be perspiring. "It was not from my camp. Never. I don't agree with anything they say in that flyer."

"Mr. Esposito," Ms. Hadley followed up, "like Mr. Ibarra, you've lived here all your life. Have you ever seen or heard anything that would lead you to believe these charges might be true?"

The councilman seemed to squirm in his seat. "I never got to know Mr. Ibarra that well," was all he could say.

In the Sandoval living room, Luis smiled and made an observation. "The guy looks like a kid caught with his hand in the cookie jar. Maybe he didn't put out the smear. But you can be sure he knew about it and hoped it would fly."

Hadley, again reporting live, went on. "I also spoke with the candidate, Emilio Ibarra, who had this to say."

Mr. Ibarra, also in a video shot earlier in the day, came on the screen. He looked cheerful with his longish black hair and big mustache. "I take all this in stride," he declared. "I'm not perfect. Who is? But my life is an open book. I have lived here in the *barrio* since I was born, and I have only one secret. A few years ago my old second-grade teacher told me if I ever run for office she is going to tell it to everybody. So here is my secret. I stole the class hamster. And I kept it at home for two days before returning it. So there it is."

When the screen went back to the anchor desk, Gloria Hadley was grinning slightly as she switched to other news.

When Ernesto went to his room to work on his report for Ms. Hunt, his phone rang.

"Ernie?" Naomi asked. "I watched Gloria Hadley. Did you? I'm hiding in my room pretending to be working on my paper. Was that a blast on the news?"

"Yeah," Ernesto chuckled. "She blew that story right out of the water. Esposito looked really guilty. I think he knows it backfired. How's your father taking it all? He's gotta be disappointed about how it's turning out."

"Oh, it's rich, Ernie," Naomi giggled. "Dad was all ready for this big exposé of Mr. Ibarra." Naomi switched to her voice imitation of her dad. "'You just watch what happens now. Those newspeople are gonna say he's all washed up now that this stuff came out.'"

Naomi chuckled, then continued in her own voice. "Then he saw his cousin up there, denouncing the flyers. He was just trying to put as much distance as he could between them and him. Dad just crumbled. Deep in his heart, I think Dad knew right along that everything in that flyer was a lie. But he was hoping against hope. Maybe some of it was true, and it would get Monte reelected."

Then Naomi's tone became serious. "You know what, Ernie? When the news program ended, Dad came to the door of my room. He was hemming and hawing. Well, real sheepish-like, he asked me if my report on 'that woman' was going okay. I think he was trying to make peace. So, you know those peanut butter cookies I make some-times, the ones Dad likes? Well, I had some left, and I was going to take them to school for my lunch. But I gave them to Dad. He smiled. He actually smiled, Ernie."

"Naomi, that's great!" Ernesto responded. "That's really great. I was so worried."

"I told you not to be, Ernie," Naomi reminded him. "Dad's a lot like Brutus. His bark is worse than his bite."

Ernesto put down the phone and started working on his F. Scott Fitzgerald report. But his thoughts were on the council race. He was determined to be active in the campaign from now on. There was no backing away from it. Ernesto was too young to vote, but he wasn't too young to campaign for Mr. Ibarra any way he could.

Monte Esposito wanted to win, and he wanted to win badly. Ernesto not only thought that he was behind the smear campaign but that maybe he had other tricks up his sleeve. That was why the *Zapatistas* had to keep the pressure on right up to election day.

At Chavez High the next day, Ernesto saw Clay Aguirre arriving. Aguirre walked over to Ernesto and said, "Don't count my man out yet, Sandoval. Remember, when you throw a little mud, some of it sticks.

Lotta people read those flyers. Now they're not so sure about Ibarra."

"You're blowin' smoke man." Ernesto replied. "Whoever put that garbage out just stunk it up for Esposito."

Naomi came up to her bike, and Clay called out to her. "Hey Naomi, you still living at home?"

Naomi laughed. "Why shouldn't I be living at home, Clay? I'm only sixteen years old."

"Dom Reynosa was telling everybody that your dad didn't want you passing out flyers for Ibarra yesterday," Clay told her. "He wanted you to come home but you refused. You made a fool of your father in front of everybody. I thought maybe he kicked you out like he did with your brothers."

"I didn't make a fool of my dad," Naomi said cooly. "I'm never disrespectful toward him. I never would be. But he wanted me to come home right away, and I needed to see Ms. Hunt."

"Dom said your old man was fightin' mad, Naomi," Clay persisted. "You better be careful. You know what happened to Orlando and Manny."

Naomi looked directly at Clay Aguirre. "Clay, everything is fine at my house. Okay? So don't you worry about it. I even gave my dad some of my super peanut butter cookies last night, and he was real happy. We all watched television then, and we saw that stupid smear campaign against Mr. Ibarra come down like a house of cards. So all in all, it was a nice evening."

For a moment, Naomi seemed as if she was done talking, but she had more to say. "And pretty soon we'll all be watching TV again on election night. And the whole *barrio* will rock like on the Fourth of July 'cause Councilman Esposito will be packing his bags and making room for a good man in that office."

Clay looked at Naomi with a half smile on his face. "Babe, admit it. Don't you sometimes wish things were different between us? Don't you remember the good old days when we had so much fun? Remember that broiling hot day in July? We went to the water park and splashed around for half the afternoon. I mean, you remember stuff like that sometimes, don't you? I sure do. You can't just wipe all those good times away."

"I haven't wiped it all away, Clay," Naomi assured him. "I'll always remember you and the times we had. It was good for most of the time. But, when it wasn't good, it was bad in a way I never want again in my life."

Clay stood there for another few seconds. Then he walked slowly away.

"He gives me the creeps," Naomi commented, as she locked up her bike. "Why can't he just move on? Mira really likes him. If he'd give her half a chance, she'd hang with him all the time. She's a pretty girl and she's nice. I wish he'd just forget about me."

"Naomi, have you ever met Clay's father?" Ernesto asked.

"Why sure, lots of times," she said. "Clay and I would go over there, and I got to know both his parents. Clay's parents are both real estate agents. They made a lot of money when houses were selling like hot cakes, but not so much lately."

"A long time ago, when me and Clay were on speaking terms," Ernesto explained, "Clay told me about his father. He said his dad is always offering advice, and Clay said he doesn't take much of it. But one thing his father told him, he said, really means something to him. He said he's taken that piece of advice to heart. 'Don't ever lose,' his father told him. 'It doesn't matter if it's sports or business. Just never lose.' I think he can't take losing you, Naomi. It's a terrible blow to his pride."

"That's pretty stupid, huh Ernie?" Naomi asked. "We're losing all the time. Sometimes it seems that's what life is all about—losing. We lose games. We lose the jobs we like. And we lose the people we love. We gotta learn to accept it. We gotta learn to cherish what's left and to make it as good as it can be. We gotta treasure what we have with all our heart and not let the losses make us bitter."

At lunchtime that day, Ernesto ate with his friends in the usual place. Abel Ruiz and Julio came first, and then Jorge and Eddie showed up. Julio seemed to have something serious on his mind, and he sat down quickly with his *burrito*.

"Listen up, you guys," Julio began. "My dad told me something last night that really rattled my cage. Dad's a street guy, you know. He hangs out with his buddies, and some of them who live down in the ravine. They talk about the wars they've been in and other stuff."

Julio looked around to make sure everyone was paying attention. "Well, there's this one dude, they call him Rezzi. Anyway, he used to work for Monte Esposito. He worked in his office. He was like a gofer for Esposito. Well, one day Rezzi refused to do some dirty work Esposito wanted done, and he got canned. When you work for Esposito, you're like the guy who walks behind the elephants in the circus parade. You gotta clean up his messes, or he fires you."

Ernesto stared at Julio, wondering where he was going. Julio was so excited he was shaking.

"This poor guy, Rezzi," Julio continued, "he's been down on his luck since he lost his job. He drinks a lot, like Dad does. He's kinda given up on life, doesn't make waves. But he comes across this smear flyer that Esposito's friends put out, the one telling lies about Ibarra. Rezzi went nuts. That's how Dad described it. Rezzi just went nuts. It brought back to him all the lousy stuff he's seen Esposito do, and how he fired Rezzi."

"Oh man," Ernesto groaned. "I bet Esposito is scared that, if he loses the election, some of his dirty deals will come out and he might be in trouble."

"You got it, dude," Julio confirmed Ernesto's thinking. "Rezzi told my dad that

Esposito's runnin' scared. He thinks maybe losing the election won't just push him out of his cushy job. It might throw light on all he's been doing—the bribes, all that. It'll be like the new guy turning the light on in the dark places. You know, like the cockroaches run when you shine a light on them. That thing about Esposito going to the island on city money, that was just the tip of the iceberg."

"How come this dude, Rezzi, doesn't go to the police or the district attorney if he has the goods on Esposito?" Ernesto asked. "If he knows something that's really big, it should come out now before the election. I think Mr. Ibarra is gonna win, but maybe not. Wouldn't it be awful if Esposito pulled it off in the end. We'd be stuck with all the corruption for another term when Rezzi could do something about it?"

"My dad, he's been telling Rezzi to blow the whistle on Esposito," Julio said, shaking his head. "Rezzi was supposed to lean on the building inspector. He was supposed to offer him money to approve a building with no steel rods in the foundation. When Rezzi balked at doing that, Esposito fired him. Rezzi's been going downhill since. Lost his wife, his kids, everything."

"Does your dad think Rezzi has enough on Esposito to make a case?" Ernesto asked.

"Yeah, for sure!" Julio affirmed.

All the boys sat quietly. They all knew what had to be done.

That night, Julio texted Ernesto that Rezzi was going to the authorities. Rezzi left word at the council's office too. He told the councilman it was all over. Rezzi was taking some documents to the district attorney. Esposito might as well concede the election right now.

Ernesto was elated and had a really good night's sleep.

CHAPTER TEN

At breakfast the next morning at the Sandoval house, Ernesto got a call on his cell. He looked away from his *huevos,* opened the phone, and said, "Yeah?" He didn't like to be interrupted during breakfast.

"He's dead man," Julio told him.

"Who's dead?" Ernesto gasped.

"Rezzi," Julio replied. "Rezzi's dead."

Ernesto felt the blood rush to his head. He felt numb and sick. He pushed himself away from the table. He got up, but his legs were almost too weak to support him. He leaned on the table, shock coursing through his body.

His family stopped eating and stared at him. They knew something was terribly wrong.

"What happened?" Ernesto finally found the voice to ask Julio.

"They found him dead in the wash," Julio answered. "He drowned man. You know we had a lot of rain last night. They're sayin' he slipped and went down into the wash. Usually it's just a trickle or it's dry. But it was running fast when Rezzi went in."

"Julio, you think—?" Ernesto gasped.

"That somebody pushed him?" Julio finished the sentence. "Maybe. I told the guy not to tell Esposito in advance. But he wanted to let the guy know what was coming down. He didn't want him to find out from the newspeople. Him drowning like that. That's a real good break for Esposito." Julio sounded bitter.

Ernesto closed the phone. Luckily, the girls hadn't gotten up yet for school. Ernesto told his parents what had happened. "This dude, Rezzi, he used to work for Esposito. He had the goods on the guy. He was planning to tell the district attorney today . . ."

A few moments of silence at the table followed. Then Maria Sandoval spoke. "I can't believe Monte Esposito would sink so low as to murder somebody. I know he's corrupt and all that, but to kill a man? Besides, how would Esposito or his people know Rezzi's plans?"

"Mom, the poor fool told Esposito last night. He told him what he planned to do," Ernesto explained.

"Uh-oh," Luis Sandoval remarked, shaking his head. "Bad move."

"We're not sure about anything," Ernesto said. "Maybe Rezzi got so upset about what he planned to do that he drank too much and slipped. When it rains hard, that ravine gets really muddy. The poor guys living there have a terrible time. Maybe he . . . just slipped."

"Esposito has a lot of people working for him," Luis Sandoval speculated. "Some aide may have gotten Rezzi's message and gone to talk to him. Maybe there was an argument. The guys who work for Esposito are going to go down with him if there's a big corruption scandal. Remember that congressman who was a big war hero, and then they uncovered a lot of corruption. He's in the slammer now, but he didn't go down alone. Other people got burned too. Maybe some aide decided he wasn't going down because of an old homeless guy who lived in the ravine."

Maria Sandoval's eyes widened. "A few years ago, down south, we had several council members on trial for taking bribes," she recalled. "Even a mayor . . . and a U.S. congressman and judges. I guess when you get into positions of power, the temptations are very strong."

"Yeah," Luis Sandoval agreed. "You get elected to serve the people, and you end up serving yourself. Greed. *Avaricia*."

Abuela had been sitting there listening quietly. Then she spoke. "My parents always taught us to never let money be your God. Never."

Luis Sandoval reached over and put his arm around his mother's shoulders. "And this is what you and Papa taught us, Mama. You taught all five of us to work hard and do the right thing."

After breakfast, Ernesto drove his Volvo to school. When he saw Julio jogging onto campus, he hailed him. "Oh man, that call this morning really shook me up. You hear anything more?"

"My dad, he got together with the veterans at the hall, Commander Sena and the others," Julio answered. "They're raising money for Rezzi's service. The military honor guard'll be there. He was a soldier. He had a good war record. Rezzi had a wife and kids, but nobody knows where they are now. We're seeing if we can't get in touch with them. Probably the wife remarried and just forgot about Rezzi."

"That's sad," Ernesto commented. "I'll see if my folks want to chip in for the burial expenses."

"Thanks, man. Every bit helps," Julio said. "Padre Benito is going to have the funeral at Our Lady of Guadalupe Church.

Rezzi didn't go there too often, usually just at Christmas, maybe Easter. But he was baptized there. It's so sad how Rezzi spent his last days livin' under a tarp. My dad is down-and-out too. But he's got his Social Security, and me and him got a room. Poor Rezzi didn't even have a home address, and he didn't even get his checks. The guy never caught a break man. Maybe thinking about all the hassle of blowing the whistle on Esposito was too much for him. Maybe he just lost it in the rain last night."

"It makes me sick," Ernesto said in disgust.

"Yeah," Julio agreed. "I told my dad it ain't gonna be that way for him, not ever. Dad's an alky like Rezzi, but he's got a son who cares about him. I'm seein' that he's okay. And when he dies, ain't nobody gonna have to beg for money for his funeral. You know, Ernie, lot of the Nam vets got a bad deal. They came home without nobody thanking them. They had emotional problems, and nobody paid any attention.

No welcome-home parades for those dudes. No thank-you-for-serving kinda stuff. Now they're getting old and dyin'. And some of them, like Rezzi, are dyin' in the rain. Somebody needs to do something for these guys."

Julio's voice broke a little, and he looked away. "That's why I'm a *Zapatista* man."

At Rezzi's funeral—his real name was David Juarez—there was no family. So the soldier gave the folded flag to Rezzi's best, and *only,* friend, Julio's father. Some of the guys from the ravine came to the funeral. They sat in the back of the church because they were dirty, and they didn't smell very good. They didn't want to offend anybody. Some veterans from the post came with Commander Sena. Julio Avila came for his father's sake. Luis Sandoval came to support his son and because, like Rezzi, he was a veteran.

Walking from the little frame church, Ernesto said, "Thanks for coming, Dad."

Luis Sandoval put his arm around his son's shoulders. "They say going to funerals like this one makes a difference.

Ernesto saw Julio walking with his father, and he waved. They came over. Julio's father was carrying a plastic bag. "All his stuff is in here," Mr. Avila explained. "I gathered it from his tarp down there. He had pictures of his kids. He told me once, if anything happened to him, I should try to find his kids and give them the pictures and a diary he kept. I guess he wrote personal stuff in there. I got a manila envelope from his tarp too. It says 'Important' on the outside."

Ernesto and his friends had two weeks before the election to canvas the neighborhoods for Emilio Ibarra. After school every day, they all walked through the *barrio* with campaign literature in their backpacks. They talked to anybody who would listen.

Not all the contacts were pleasant. A woman on Cardinal Street told Ernesto that she was supporting Monte Esposito. He'd been in the job so long, she asserted, he knew how to do it. Besides, Ibarra looked like a fool with that big mustache.

Ernesto didn't argue with anybody. He was cheerful and pleasant even to the man who told him that all politicians were crooks anyway and that it didn't matter whom you voted for. Ernesto thanked the man for listening to him and moved on.

An elderly woman on Tremayne took the brochure that showed the smiling Ibarra. She frowned and asked, "Why is he laughing? He looks like a clown. We don't need a clown in the city council. It's already a circus."

"Oh, he's actually a very serious man," Ernesto explained, "but he likes to smile and make people happy."

"Oh, so he *is* a clown," the woman sniffed before handing the flyer back and moving on.

Some of the people Ernesto talked to were registered to vote, but they didn't plan to vote in this election.

"I just vote when the president is up," a man declared.

"Sometimes city councilmen have more effect on our lives than the president," Ernesto told him, handing the man a flyer.

"I'd like to know what the city council does that matters to me," the man asked.

"They decide how many police officers and firefighters we have," Ernesto answered. "They manage the libraries. They fix the potholes and make intersections safer by putting in traffic lights."

"Oh," the man said. "I didn't know that. Then maybe I will vote for—this guy Ibarra?"

"That would be good!" Ernesto affirmed.

Whenever Ernesto was finished walking the streets for the day, his feet hurt and he was tired. And then some days he had to go work at the pizzeria.

One night, when Ernesto got home from work, his father was working on the computer, preparing tests for his history classes.

"I'm worn out!" Ernesto declared, collapsing onto the sofa. "I walked around for a couple hours talking to people about the election. Then I was dishing up pizzas. But, you know what, Dad? It's kinda exciting to be part of something like this. I've never been involved in an election before, and it's kinda cool."

Luis Sandoval smiled. "Yes, when you feel passionate about something, you find the energy, no matter how tired you feel."

"The polls are looking good, Dad," Ernesto told him. "I think we're gonna win. Man, election night will be so exciting. I can hardly wait. Me and Naomi are going over to the Ibarra house for the big celebration."

Ernesto's father looked a little troubled. "How is Naomi's father dealing with all this?" he asked. "I mean, with his daughter campaigning against his cousin, his friend."

"I think he's kinda accepting it, Dad," Ernesto answered. "I was kinda surprised by him. When Naomi stood up to her father, he didn't go ballistic. I think he loves her very much."

"Ernie," Mr. Sandoval said, "I meant to tell you . . . Today at school, Julio brought me an envelope from Rezzi's property. The envelope was filled with what looked like legal papers. They involved city transactions. I'm a history teacher, not a lawyer. So I didn't understand all that was there. I asked my brother, your Uncle Arturo, to look at the stuff. Arturo is a lawyer, and he'll know what he's looking at. Maybe Rezzi had some assets we don't know about and he wanted to leave them to someone."

"Yeah, that's good, Dad," Ernesto acknowledged. "Julio is still searching the Internet for Rezzi's kids."

"Arturo said he'd be looking too," Dad said. "Poor Rezzi, didn't have much of a life, but at least he had a decent burial. I was glad the veterans came. They never forget their own."

"Yeah," Ernesto agreed.

"So, go to bed and get some sleep, *mi hijo,*" Mr. Sandoval commanded with a smile. "Who knows? Perhaps all this politicking will get into your blood. Maybe someday you may decide to be a lawyer, and then a politician too."

Ernesto laughed. "I don't think so, Dad. It's too dirty a business. I couldn't handle that. Look how they tried to smear Mr. Ibarra."

"*Mi hijo,*" Mr. Sandoval advised, "politics will always be as dirty as the men and women who participate in it. If good, honorable men and women get elected, then it won't be dirty anymore."

"Maybe," Ernesto conceded, heading for the shower. But as the hot water splashed over his tired body, he had a strange thought. Maybe he *should* consider going into law and then politics. *Representative* Ernesto Sandoval? *Senator* Ernesto Sandoval? Ernesto laughed to himself. The idea was ridiculous. No, he would become a teacher like his father. Dad did so much good as a teacher. Ernesto could too, but still . . .

A fantasy came to mind. "*President* Ernesto Sandoval, the first Hispanic president of the United States, is now taking the oath of office." He chuckled at the mental image.

Usually, whenever the president or governor or senators were not on the ballot, the election turnout was small. That was typically the case all over the city, and the *barrio* was no exception. When only city council candidates and a few propositions that people didn't understand anyway were on the ballot, a handful of people trickled to the polls.

But not this time. On this election day, Ernesto noticed quite a few people making their way to the polling places. Some were even lined up before seven when the polls were due to open. That was unusual. At Cesar Chavez High School, one of the polling places, signs directed voters to the library, where everything was set up. A flag stood at the door with a list of voters who belonged in that precinct.

Ernesto was pretty sure Emilio Ibarra would win, but one never knew. You couldn't be totally sure. The smear seemed to have backfired, but maybe some people still wondered whether the accusations were true. Maybe they would go into that booth and choose the safe name, the one they recognized—the incumbent, Monte Esposito. He was the devil most people knew. And he was better than the devil they didn't know, Emilio Zapata Ibarra.

Ernesto was on edge all day. He found it hard to concentrate on his classes. He kept looking at his phone and checking the time. How many hours were left until the polls closed? When would the returns come in? Luckily, he thought, election day was a Tuesday. He didn't have to work tonight.

When the last bell of the day rang, Ernesto went to the parking lot to wait for

Naomi to take her home. Then, around eight o'clock, he'd pick her up and take her to the Ibarra house. There would, of course, be a victory celebration downtown at the Ibarra headquarters if he won. But Ernesto and Naomi wanted to be part of the celebration on Nuthatch Lane. Ernesto and the other neighbors would share Conchita's homemade *posole* and Mexican hot chocolate. Then, much later, Emilio Ibarra would make his acceptance speech downtown, which would be carried on local television.

The first returns were the absentee ballots. They came in early, right after the polls closed, and they were mixed. Ibarra was leading, but not by much.

Naomi, Ernesto, and about twenty other people waited in the Ibarra house for the returns. They hoped the trend would be established early, and it was. Emilio Ibarra surged ahead. As he did, wild cheers exploded from the people in the Ibarra living room. Carmen's voice was the loudest. She and her mother grabbed each other and danced around the living room. With every announcement of the election results, Ibarra's margin of victory increased. It was beginning to look like a landslide. Cheers and yells filled the small house on Nuthatch Lane. It was becoming more and more certain that the next councilman from the *barrio* would be Emilio Zapata Ibarra.

Ernesto hugged Naomi, and they both hugged Carmen.

After the celebration, when Ernesto dropped Naomi home, the Martinez house was very quiet. Ernesto gave Naomi a long kiss. Then she whispered, "I'm going to sneak in very quietly. Goodnight, Ernie." She giggled and danced up the walk to her door.

When Ernesto got home, he shouted, "We did it!" He was grinning from ear to ear. The local news was telecasting Monte Esposito's concession speech, followed by Emilio Ibarra's very humble acceptance speech. Mr. Ibarra promised to work with all his heart and soul for all the people in his district. In an emotional voice, he pledged to be a true servant of the people.

"I believe him," Ernesto's father stated fervently.

"Yes," Maria Sandoval agreed.

Ernesto's father clicked off the television set, stood, and came over to Ernesto. He had a very serious look on his face.

"*Tío* Arturo called me, Ernie. The manila envelope contains evidence— shocking evidence of long-term corruption in Esposito's office. Favors were exchanged for substantial bribes. Arturo is turning everything over to the district attorney."

As Ernesto went down the hallway to his room, he felt both sad and triumphant. He wasn't sure whether Rezzi fell or was pushed into those dark swirling floodwaters the night he died. He might never know. But if Rezzi had died trying to expose corruption, then at least he didn't die in vain. Like the good soldier he was, he up-held his principles even from the grave.

Ernesto showered, toweled off, and got into his pajamas. He glanced at himself in the mirror, with his black hair wet and water still shimmering on his skin. Suddenly the whole world seemed to be open to him. The most improbable dreams seemed within his reach. Maybe not likely, but possible. All a man or woman needs to pursue such dreams is courage. The courage of conviction. The courage to go forward, even against impossible odds.

Dad was a man of courage. Once gang-bangers threw a chunk of concrete through the window of the Sandoval house. They meant to threaten Dad because he was trying to get dropouts off the street and back into school. But Luis Sandoval never backed off. He kept doing what he needed to do. That took courage.

Even Naomi showed more courage. Sure, Ernesto encouraged her to stand up to her dad. But she was the one who had to walk through the door and face him. And she did. That took courage too.

Ernesto winced a bit when he thought about his own lack of courage. He wimped out of becoming a *Zapatista* because he was afraid of losing Naomi. It took the outrage of the smear flyers for him to see what he had to do.

"Well," Ernesto declared to himself, "*basta*! There are times *for* courage. And, from now on, I must make them times *of* courage."